A COURAGEOUS BETROTHAL

SCOUTS OF THE GEORGIA FRONTIER
BOOK TWO

DENISE WEIMER

WILD HEART
BOOKS

Cover design by Evelyne Labelle at Carpe Librum Book Design. www.carpelibrumbookdesign.com

ISBN-13: 978-1-942265-72-6

PRAISE FOR A COURAGEOUS
BETROTHAL

PROLOGUE

LATE JUNE, 1778
WILKES COUNTY, GEORGIA

She first sensed someone watching as a prickle of awareness on the back of her neck as she and Hester floated, shift-clad, in the creek. Even in the cool waters, the fine ginger hairs from Jenny White's nape to her arms stirred, and she froze.

Casting a glance over her shoulder, she saw him—a brown bare-chested native, his face smeared with black-and-red war paint. He did not even attempt to conceal himself. After all, the White family may have brought their livestock out from Augusta and built a cabin four years prior. They might have planted their small patches of corn, wheat, and flax alongside the vegetable garden Jenny and her sister had been weeding in the fork of Long and Dry Fork Creeks before yielding to the urge to cool down from the sun's blistering rays. But this had been his land. Whether Hitchiti Creek of the first people in these parts, or Muskogee who came from the west many years ago, he belonged and she did not.

But the brave's alliance with the British made him Jenny's enemy. She was old enough to remember from North Carolina what the British could do. She had given up too much—her little brother's life and her best years to make a good match, for starters—to just hand over this land.

Thank God Gabriel had not taken the Brown Bess hunting today. She'd left it propped against the giant oak that marked the ford. With the steady diagonal trajectory of a water bug, she waded toward Hester and the tree.

Hester's head—curly strawberry-blond hair darkened and dripping—broke the surface. She started to let out an exclamation of delight but gave only a gasp when Jenny's firm hand encircled her wrist. Green eyes wide, she allowed herself to be towed toward the shore.

"Hester, run for the house. Make sure Ma and the baby stay inside."

The younger girl's eyes trained on the forest and

found the focus of Jenny's concern. "Oh, dear Jesus, please save us," she whispered.

"Jesus saves those who save themselves."

Hester had started to shake like a Quaker overcome by the Spirit. And for good reason. Just last summer, she'd watched Thomas Dooly, a seasoned officer, die at this very spot from a wound inflicted by a member of Creek Chief Emistisiguo's war party. Attempted revenge for that death had sent Thomas's brother John, now their new county's representative, to a court martial. And it had led their father to construct a loop-holed stockade, rude but surmounted with lookouts at each angle, around his cabin and outbuildings last fall.

But now their father fought in Florida under their neighbor, Lieutenant Colonel Elijah Clark. And John Dooly, still bent on vengeance for his brother's death, again commanded troops as a colonel of Wilkes County militia. With his men out against other Creek raiders, and Hester's twin, Gabriel, not yet fourteen, hoeing corn furrows for a neighbor soldier's wife, the fort house offered pitiful protection to the White women. A few burning arrows could reduce it to ashes in a matter of minutes.

In her gut, Jenny knew only a bold and fearless show of strength might save them. But first, she had to get Hester out of view.

She shoved her pretty sister from the water. "Run. Bolt the stockade door."

Hester cowered on the bank, covering her dripping shift with her arms. "Not without you!"

"One gun on the lookout could never hold them off. We only stand a chance if I show we do not fear them. Now go." Hopefully, her voice conveyed a bravado she did not feel. Jenny stood to her full, wiry height of almost six feet, red hair hanging unbound down her back.

"Have you taken leave of your senses?" Hester gasped.

Another Indian moved into view, finally startling Hester to flight.

Jenny heard the fort door close but never took her eyes off her adversaries. Palm up, she extended a hand toward the forest and said in a calm but loud voice, "We have no fight if you leave in peace. But I will defend this land if I must."

The first Indian did not move. The second, crouched behind a hickory, notched an arrow.

Jenny's legs started quivering like a newborn colt's. *Oh God, Father, hold me up. Send us the protection of Thy mighty angels.*

The next moment, what felt like a large insect brushed her thigh. She looked down at a ragged tear in her shift left by the Indian's arrow. Jenny gritted her teeth, sudden anger unfurling from her middle and rushing up in a bellow of protest. What cowardly man shot a lone woman standing next-to-naked on a creek bank?

Jenny took one long step and had fourteen pounds of Brown Bess in her hand. She had already rammed powder, ball, and wadding up to the breech. As she crouched behind the oak, the first brave simply watched her, but war whoops echoed among the trees. She pulled back on the dogshead to cock the weapon and gazed down the barrel.

If she killed the brave who tested her now, the others would kill her and overrun the fort. If she did nothing, they would still overrun the fort. In a flash, she noticed the long tree branch extending above the man's roached and feathered head. She sighted from breech pin to muzzle as Father had taught her when they bark-chipped squirrels out of trees. She had always been a better shot than Gabriel, preserving the most meat possible. May God preserve them today.

Jenny fired. The brave did not even duck until the branch almost hit him. She plastered herself against the tree as a din of yells and shots rose.

She did not look, just prayed. And reloaded. Fast. Jenny had two choices—kill as many as possible as they forded the creek in hopes that Gabriel might hear the ruckus and return before they had their way with

Mother, Hester, and Libby...or raise the muzzle to her own head and spare herself the certain horrors to come.

Suddenly, a voice of command rang out. "*Wahatchee.*"

Following another sharp order, silence fell.

CHAPTER 1

JANUARY 1, 1779

Scarcely after midnight, Jenny had just settled into a slumber as decent as the cold loft allowed when a pounding on the cabin door made her sit bolt upright. Beside her, Hester levered to a similar right angle. On the floor beneath them, from the one-legged bed, their mother gasped, "Asa, get the gun!"

Gabriel scrambled down the ladder, and their parents scuffled around below, loading the musket and igniting a stick of fatwood in the banked embers of the hearth. Hester's small-boned, chilly hand slid over to tangle with Jenny's. "Well, it cannot be Indians," Hester whispered. "Else they would have already tomahawked the door down."

"No, but perchance someone fleeing them."

They counted their June escape a miracle. Settlers puzzled over the strange markings that appeared on the fork tree at the Whites' the morning after the incident, conjecturing that Jenny's bravery had earned the Indians' protection. To her chagrin, she had become something of a local legend. That fall, word came that Creek Indians destroyed two county forts, McNabb's and Nail's. Now people scurried for the safety of Fort White's walls at the slightest provocation.

"Who goes there?" their father's voice boomed.

The cheer of the reply belied the scolding words. "Yer fellow hatchet man, freezin' his rear off. Will ye not admit me and me friends from this cold?"

"It cannot be!"

The musket's stock thumped softly on the floorboards installed only a month ago. They both lunged for the edge of the loft as their father slid up the bolt. In the low light of the burning brand, he offered a back-thumping embrace to a large, tall form, while several other shapes stood silhouetted in the moonlight behind.

"Happy Hogmanay!" the newcomer exclaimed.

"Whist, man, where did you come from? You cannot have been lurking about the wilderness for the sole purpose of crossing my threshold first on your silly Scottish holiday!"

"From Fort Martin, and the wilds beyond." The tall man swept his arm behind him. "But I do admit to using the moonlight to my advantage to claim 'first foot.'"

"Do you bring good luck or bad?" Father questioned as he took a step back inside, but Jenny could hear the grin in his voice.

"A mixture, I warrant. On such a dire mission, I lack the traditional gifts, but I do have a packet of salt on my horse." He drew out a silver flask that winked in the pale light. "And this, in hopes you will share your hearth."

Jenny's mother shuffled about said aperture, removing the curfew from the coals and spreading them with her poker, while Gabriel lingered nearby in the awkward waiting stance of youth.

"Dire?" Father's voice lowered, dropping the teasing edge. He waved the men in. "Come in, Caylan, and all your friends. Welcome. Tell us your mission and how we can help."

Hester pinched Jenny's arm, demanding her attention. "He called him *Caylan*. Jenny, I think he be the McIntosh."

"The McIntosh?" In the noise of the travelers divesting themselves of guns and accoutrements and settling onto benches around the smooth-drawn boards Gabriel brought from the wall and laid over the trestles,

Jenny fumbled for her wool over-petticoat. "Even if he is the Caylan McIntosh Father speaks so highly of, he would hardly be 'the McIntosh.' I durst say that honor would be due to his grandfather or great uncle or one of the other older and more important heads of that clan near Savannah."

"What are you doing?"

"Getting dressed. They are bound to be hungry." She grabbed her apron from its peg and tied the laces.

Hester's exasperated look said Jenny always demanded to be in the middle of any action. Jenny did not wait for her scolding but pushed aside the bearskin that separated her brother's corner of the loft from theirs and wiggled down the ladder. She landed with a thud just as Father introduced his friend to Gabriel, causing the man's head to swivel in her direction.

His look of surprise was nothing new to Jenny. She towered over most men, intimidating and alarming them with her bright-red hair and sturdy frame, but not this one. No, this one was over six feet himself, and the look he gave her...could it be admiration? At the notion, embarrassment licked its way from her toes to her scalp, making her cheeks heat.

Father gave a sigh. "This is my eldest, Jenny." As the buckskin-clad arrival reached for her hand and gave a slight bow, he added, "Meet Caylan McIntosh, Jenny, the crazy Scot I told you about."

In the firelight Mother had managed to resurrect, Caylan's hair, clubbed with twine, glowed like the rich mahogany of a wealthy merchant's sideboard Jenny admired once in Augusta. When he spoke, his voice was teasing. "And what, pray, did he tell you of me?"

He still held her hand. She pulled back. "He said that you led the charge at the Battle of Alligator Bridge and broke your horse's leg trying to leap the last ditch separating you from the British regulars."

The light left those amber-tinged brown eyes. "Dinna think that was my choosing, lass. He was a good horse. When I realized the ditch was purposely dug too wide, 'twas too late. I have never wished to make mince-feet of anyone so bad as I did those red-coated maca-ronis that day."

Father shook his head. "And yet Clark called the retreat."

"He had little choice." Caylan lifted one of his thick shoulders. "They had us hemmed in, and Clark himself was wounded."

"I was never so glad as to get my husband back from that campaign." With a clatter, Mother replaced the poker in its holder and brushed off her hands, turning toward them with her eyes glinting. "And I hope he never has to repair to the tangled swamps of Florida again."

"Well, ma'am, 'tis not to Florida I would take him, but Savannah."

"Savannah?" she asked. "Why?"

"The city has fallen."

A feminine gasp from the loft caused Caylan to look upward. A dark shape moved out of the light, and he continued.

"General Howe, uncertain where the British would land once their ships were sighted, spread out his troops. When a slave led part of the landing party through the swamp to flank him, he lost eighty-three killed and eleven wounded."

"Oh no," Mother murmured. She knew what this meant, that she would lose her husband again, prematurely, before spring even greened the trees.

Distress written on his gently lined features, Father turned to Jenny. "You should go back upstairs to bed."

"I came down to help Mother." Jenny moved to her mother's side. Besides, nothing could prevent her from hearing the rest of Caylan's news now. They would have to drag her back up the ladder, and she doubted any of them were strong enough to do so, save Caylan himself. While her father was built sturdy, the three-month stints of militia service over the last few years had left him worn, shadowed.

"Oh, ma'am, we's not expectin' victuals at this hour," one of the men protested.

His burlier companion elbowed him. "Speak for yerself. I ain't et since we left Cherokee Corner."

"My Elizabeth will see that all are satisfied." Their father shot their mother a warm glance.

She nodded, then whispered to Jenny as she nudged her toward the sideboard. "We can heat yesterday's cornmeal mush." Under her mobcap and silvering corkscrew curls, her eyes told Jenny both of her gratefulness for her daughter's assistance and her concern over what the family themselves would now have to break their fast.

Jenny sought the butter bowl as Mother placed her short-legged iron spider over the heat.

The men settled around the table. "Is Clark at Woburn now?" her father asked.

He referred to their neighbor's plantation, now fortified and known as Clark's Station, about eight miles east on Red Lick Creek, another fork of Long Creek. After recovering from his Florida campaign wound at Sunbury, south of Savannah, Clark had returned to the care of his wife, Hannah. But the lieutenant colonel had likely already mobilized in the face of this new aggression.

Caylan confirmed it. "Clark's regiment musters across the river at Fort Charlotte. He sent me and several other scouts into the backcountry to gather new recruits and those on leave. You have met the

Morris brothers here from across the Oconee. Philip Dunst of Scull Shoals is stabling the horses. He'll be in in a few minutes. Others will come. I thought to stay until dawn to set out for Clark Station, then on to South Carolina."

"By all means," Father agreed. "And the enemy?"

Jenny listened intently to the men's now-low voices as she fried the mush over the fire. Though she knew better than to give any man a second glance, Caylan McIntosh commanded the room. Scout or no, he clearly hailed from warrior stock.

"The Georgia banks of the Savannah River are controlled by a Loyalist force under Colonel Daniel McGirth. We expect Campbell in Savannah to be reinforced and make Augusta his next conquest. The lobsters think to find their own recruits in these parts, to turn the war against us."

Father's arm thumped on the table. "So we take the fight to them."

"Aye. Can we count on ye, Asa White?"

"You know I am always there for Clark. And even his Sawny neighbor on the Broad."

Surprised to hear her normally straight-laced parent—since her youth in North Carolina a convert to the New Light Baptist persuasion—use a slang term for a Scotsman, Jenny glanced up as her father sat back from the table with a wink and a half smirk. Somehow, this McIntosh brought out his youthful, mischievous side.

The same, however, could not be said of her mother. No one but Jenny saw the grimace that twisted her dainty features at her husband's military commitment. It vanished by the time the stout, short German, Dunst, entered, seated himself at the table, and accepted his hostess's offer of cider.

He swiveled around to acknowledge her. "Thank you, ma'am. I am plumb chapt."

Mother offered a stiff smile as she reached for the wooden trenchers on the shelf. After slicing a portion of salted fish onto each, she came to kneel by Jenny. "Almost ready, daughter?"

Wrapping the iron spider's handle with a rag, Jenny moved it forward. "Yes."

Mother passed her the plates as Jenny served with a spatula.

Gabriel's voice came, pitched almost as low as his elders'. "Father, I wish to go with you."

Mother's head jerked around, and Jenny steadied the plate she held out.

"Nae, son, you are too young," Father replied.

"How old are ye, boy?" Caylan studied him with narrowed eyes.

Gabriel raised his chin, as yet untouched by any hint of a beard. "Fourteen."

Caylan gave a slow nod. "There are some in the regiment of that age."

Mother stood and scowled. "Not my son. Who would protect us at Fort White?"

Gabriel's gaze turned their way as Jenny rose from the hearth and brushed off her skirts. "Jenny."

At the guffaw that issued from one of the Morris brothers, telltale color heated her cheeks again. Gabriel did not help by continuing, "You all know she shoots better than I do, can hoe a straighter row, and even knows how to tan hides. She is no stranger to hard work—"

Father's command cut off his son's sentence. "Gabriel, that will be enough."

"Mayhap we ought to enlist the sister, Lieutenant," the older, taller Morris observed, leaning a shoulder into Caylan's.

Father continued as if he had not spoken, his gaze on Gabriel. "I could not do my duty knowing I left my womenfolk alone in the wilderness. You will remain and man this fort house."

Her brother hung his head and released a quiet breath of frustration.

"Many civilians are fleeing to safety in the Carolinas," the German told them.

Jenny put her hands on her hips and spoke without hesitation. "We shan't flee."

When her father nodded, she moved toward the table with two plates. As she slid them onto the board, Caylan's hand shot out, his strong, warm fingers curling around her arm. She darted a look at his face, her heart skittering to her stockinged toes as their gazes tangled. "Lass. Something tells me you must be Wahatchee."

"*What?*" Jenny had not forgotten the word the warrior in the forest had bellowed across the creek. She had just never thought to hear it again.

"The carved letters on the trunk of the tree that stands at the river's fork—they spell *Wahatchee*. And there is also a sign instructing travelers to pass by the land in peace."

She placed a hand over her galloping heart. "There is?"

Caylan nodded. Though the others watched, Jenny could not look away from the Scotsman.

"What does it mean?"

A slow grin creased the corners of his mouth. "War Woman."

CHAPTER 2

*C*aylan's words, "others will come," came to fulfillment. All that day, men and boys slipped into the White compound. Gabriel tended the many horses overflowing their humble stable. Some of the men went hunting and returned with a couple of turkeys that kept Jenny and her mother busy dressing and baking. Hester slipped into the role of hostess, drifting among the men with tankards of cider. They treated her with tender respect, as though she was a grand English lady. Jenny gritted her teeth at the way Caylan's eyes followed Hester's softly rounded girlish form, laced into her best winter petticoat and stays, her golden curls trailing from beneath her cap.

She was used to it. She was. The frontier had just made her forget a little. The frontier flipped things backward, making a strong, tough girl desirable and a weak, delicate one a liability. But the presence of men always managed to put things back in their natural order.

"What are they doing outside?" Hester stopped to ask Caylan as he sat before their fire oiling his fine Kentucky rifle.

He glanced up with a smile. "Building a bonfire to celebrate Hogmanay. Your father approved it."

"Even though we employ prayers to keep evil spirits at bay," Mother put in from the board where she kneaded the supper bread, "and have no need of fire."

"Aye, 'tis just for fun. We even have a fiddler among us for a bit of music and dancing."

Jenny paused in greasing the bread pan. Dancing? How long had it been since she'd gallivanted through the steps of a reel? Since she'd been a child, no doubt. To cover her lapse, she hurried over to restack the homemade wooden blocks her youngest sister, Liberty, almost three, knocked down.

"I hope your men are keen on dancing with each other," Mother retorted with a soft snort. "You know my husband does not hold with such diversion."

"I am aware of his persuasion, which I believe comes from your time at Sandy Creek?"

"That is correct. The first time Mister White heard Reverend Stearns preach, he left his Congregationalist background behind." She shook her head, her eyes losing their focus. "I have never heard a man speak with such fire."

Jenny still remembered the sermons that had drawn settlers from the Yadkin River Valley, up to forty miles away, to the Sandy Creek Baptist Church. She had puzzled a long time over the "new birth" the dynamic preacher referred to. Finally, her mother explained it meant giving her life to Christ and allowing the power of the Holy Spirit, the third member of the Godhead, to enable her to put off the "old Jenny" and live as a "new Jenny." She had agreed to that, but over the years, "old Jenny" seemed to keep emerging.

"Then, madam, ye must not have heard the address of Elijah Clark." With a smile that made Jenny's blood pause in its courses, Caylan put away his cleaning rag and fixed the ramrod of his rifle.

"Oh, 'tis different. I speak of religious fervor, although I own, what we experienced during the Regulator Rebellion stirred my husband's patriotism."

"I have heard of the rebellion against Governor Tryon's unfair taxation."

"Oh dear. Your mitten needs mending." Hester fingered a pulled thread on the knit half glove on Caylan's right hand.

Basting the surface of Mother's bread with melted butter, Jenny frowned

Caylan smiled at Hester. "I was just going to see to that. See here, I have my mending kit." He dug in his haversack.

"Never mind, I will get my sewing needle. A soldier must not concern himself with such trivials."

As though knitting and simple work were so very exhausting. Stifling a snort, Jenny carried the bread to the beehive oven built into one side of their chimney. As she situated the loaf with a long-handled shovel, Mother flashed her a sympathetic look, to which Jenny turned up the corners of her mouth.

While her younger daughter went to fetch her sewing kit, Mother began to clean the board. "As we were saying, Lieutenant McIntosh," she resumed, "not only unfair taxation, including using monies intended for public schools to build his palatial mansion, but repression of the worst kind. Much as it is here, the inland settlers resented the coastal aristocrats occupying all the positions of political power. Separate Baptists and Quakers saw alike on that and formed the Regulators."

"Did not the Regulators use violence to make themselves heard?" Caylan cocked his head, frowning.

Hester returned and drew his mitten off with gentle fingers and gentle smile. Jenny's stomach turned sour as the brine they sometimes used to pickle meat.

"Some did, although Shubal Stearns did not sanction violence. But when the governor raised troops to form a militia against the Regulators, we all united. Doubtless, you have heard of the Battle of Alamance, in seventy-one?"

Caylan sipped his cider. "I have."

"A hundred and fifty wounded, twenty dead. Six Regulators hanged. Tryon sent troops to Sandy Creek to find those in hiding, burned crops and farms, forced oaths to be signed. Most left the area."

"Did Asa join that fight?" Caylan's tone showed this came as a surprise. "He never mentioned it."

Mother shook her head. "In light of the fact that we lived closer to the Yadkin, and he had a young family, my husband only supported the Regulators in principle. But after that, things changed. And when we heard of the new land opening up in this area..."

"A fresh start." Caylan nodded.

On the floor under the table, Libby scattered her blocks and started to cry. Jenny bent to lift her.

"Here, you are busy. Set her on my knee for a horsey ride." Caylan patted the leg of his breeches.

Jenny paused and blinked at him. Most men wanted nothing to do with babies, especially those not their own. "Have you little siblings too?" She ventured a step in his direction but still clasped her sister against her.

"Sure an' I have, siblings and cousins aplenty. You can trust me. I shan't spill her."

Jenny lowered her sister onto Caylan's muscular thigh.

"What's her name?"

"Liberty, since she was born in seventy-six. We call her Libby."

"Ah, a fittin' moniker, that one. Hello, Libby." Lightening his voice, Caylan leaned over to tweak the babe's button nose.

Jenny hovered a moment to ensure cries of protest did not break forth. Instead, as the lieutenant began to talk to the little girl and waggle her up and down, her face wreathed in smiles. A longing rose in Jenny's heart that she promptly squashed, asking, "Did Father say all your family remains on the coast?"

"Aye. My grandfather came over from Inverness to found New Inverness, what's now known as Darien, in 1736, with Highlanders recruited to hold off the Indians and Spanish from swarming north to Sunbury and Savannah. He was killed at the Battle of Bloody Marsh."

"How remarkable." Hester's needles paused. "Do the Scots still dress in their native way?"

"Yes, my family wears the *feileadh mhor* and *brogs* and carry their broadswords and targes. And of course, Brown Bess muskets." Caylan grinned.

"Why do you not?"

"Though I donned my breeches for today's festivities, I find buckskin and leggings much more practical —and subtler—on the frontier." He gave Hester a wink.

She flushed prettily, not like the pulsing red that frequented Jenny's face.

Jenny rested her hand on her hip, cocking her head. "What made you leave the coast?"

Caylan looked up at her. "You see before you a maverick, Mistress White, one who prefers quiet to clamor and the solitary to the clan. A Scottish anomaly."

His words pierced her. Had she not often felt the same way? As though she stuck out like a sore thumb in this White family? In this English family? She bit her lip and nodded.

Caylan broke her gaze, glanced at Hester as he placed a finger on a hammered metal pin at his waist. "I do wear this, though. The clan brooch with the cat-a-mountain."

While Hester murmured her admiration and Caylan brushed a stray curl out of her face so that she could see, Jenny turned away. No need to countenance the inevitable.

*a*s dusk fell and the bonfire in the clearing was lit, Caylan joined his men tossing torches and telling stories. Gabriel escorted Jenny to the river to wash trenchers, causing her to eye the singing, laughing, recumbent linsey-woolsey and buckskin forms around the popping orange flames with longing. But when, hands chapped numb, they returned to the cabin, their mother paused her sweeping long enough to fix them both with a piercing eye.

"Put it from your minds," she said.

"I have to feed the livestock and the soldiers' horses, Mother," Gabriel pointed out in a dry tone.

Jenny hastened to add, "There are so many, he will need help."

"Fine, but the minute you hear Old Scratch's fiddle, hasten inside. I fear some of those men have been much in their cups."

Jenny could not tell if Caylan McIntosh was one of those. Judging by the volume of the tale she overheard from the livestock pen, it seemed possible.

"'We sir, are fighting the battle of America and therefore disdain to remain neutral,' my good cousin wrote." Caylan stood to give the words greater effect, his form silhouetted against the bonfire as Jenny forked hay to the horses.

"'The battle of America,' what brass," someone exclaimed.

"Wait, it gets better." Caylan pointed a finger at the recruit. "The good lieutenant colonel in charge of Fort Morris then stated, 'as to surrendering the Fort receive this reply, *Come and take it!*'"

Hoots, laughter, and cries of "come and take it!" reverberated throughout the stockade. You would have thought the Patriot Highlanders and Howe's troops had mowed down the British ranks of Lord Cornwallis himself. But the fighting spirit of the militia encouraged her. She knew how these men fought—laying ambushes, tracking and traveling long distances in record time like the Indians. Once they drew the British regulars into the backcountry, the red-heeled fops wouldn't stand a chance.

The unseen fiddler took his cue. The notes anchored themselves inside Jenny's chest, with invisible strings tugging her toward the sound. Caylan and presumably several other Scots started a jig. From his fancy footwork and agile leaps, the lieutenant appeared dead sober. She found herself propping the pitchfork against a wall and drifting closer in the shadows, her mother's previous warning drowned out in the waterfall of lilting notes.

When the musician warbled into "Soldier's Joy," a woman faced off with her husband. As they greeted and turned, two frontiersmen leapt up to join them. Caylan looked around as though searching for a partner and noticed Jenny standing just outside the circle of light. He came toward her, hand outstretched.

"Come, lass, will ye dance with me? Ye know this one."

Indeed, she did. She had seen settlers perform the steps on the Yadkin River. Before Jenny had time to think, Caylan whirled her into the circle, and a man dancing a female part grabbed her for a ladies' chain. She caught a brief glimpse of Gabriel's alarmed face as she whizzed past.

Delighted with the actual women who joined them, the men paid courtly attention that caused Jenny's face to flame. But none more than the sensation of Caylan's eyes, warm amber in the firelight, fixed on her every time they met. The roughened strength of his large hand made hers feel small.

When the song changed, Jenny gave an awkward curtsy and tried to back away, but her partner caught her arm. "'Tis just a Cumberland Reel."

"I know no Cumberland Reel. Remember, we do not dance."

"Oh. I did forget that." But Caylan's smirk hinted otherwise. "Seems to me Wahatchee would not grow lily-livered at a wee promenade. See, 'tis only a skip step, toe to heel?"

Jenny turned her lips down. "Wahatchee has a mother."

Caylan threw his head back and laughed. "What? That slip of a woman has a Highland princess like you all a'cower?"

"I am English, sir." She clasped her hands behind her petticoats.

"Well, pardon me, my lady," he retorted with mock offense, "but yer regal bearing and coloring beg otherwise. I wager some hint of Celtic besmears the White family past...far back in the recesses of time, no doubt."

The "regal coloring" went up in flames. Jenny repeated what she'd heard her mother proudly state many times. "We come from pure English stock."

"Well, then, I dare ye to prove a proper English lady has no fear of a Cumberland Reel."

"Those are break teeth words, McIntosh. If I chose, I could dance until daybreak, and still be dancing long after you collapse." So saying, Jenny stalked to the tail of the reel and waited for the laughing Scotsman to follow her.

Just like firing a gun, riding a horse, clearing brush, and swimming, dancing provided no challenge. Jenny did all physical things well and with endurance. What she had not expected, however, was the way Caylan's obvious approval made her feel. It answered a craving deep inside that she had attempted to discredit for years. Not to mention the brush of his fingertips, the pressure of his hand on her waist, spread the bonfire to her bones.

Jenny stood off to one side as he went to get cider, fighting the urge to flee before he glimpsed admiration on her face. She would be twenty this spring, too old for girlish fantasies. She heard the Morris brothers talking in front of her.

"Think I shall see if I can steal the ginger-pated wench from McIntosh. A hearty girl like that could bear some strong sons."

"No doubt, brother, if you look the other way as you bed her."

Raucous laughter, elbowing, and spilled cider accompanied the remark that punched like a mule's hoof to Jenny's chest. She had already started for the cabin when she noticed her parents pressing into the celebration, worried faces portent of coming ill. Good. She could slip around behind them and climb up into bed. As for Caylan, she could avoid him when the troop departed at dawn.

He might admire her spirit and strength, but when it came to picking the wife he would want to wake to every morning, like the Morris brothers, like all men, he would choose a Hester over a Jenny every time.

CHAPTER 3

*J*enny's back ached. She paused to rub it, standing upright to survey Gabriel tugging a repaired log onto the split-rail fence surrounding the potato and corn patch where she spread manure from a homemade barrow. Her eye caught a moving form on the path across the river.

Calling her brother, she nodded toward the gun propped nearby. He had just palmed the musket when the rider came into view. Jenny released her anxiety in a puff of breath. There might just be some delight in that sigh too.

She hurried to Gabriel's side and waved. After Caylan's brown stallion splashed across the creek, Jenny called, "Lieutenant McIntosh! Do you bring us news?"

They had seen and heard little since the troop departed in early January, a month and some ten days now.

"Aye, Miss White, and not of the good variety." He swung down with the ease of long legs but the stiffness of endless hours spent in the saddle. Caylan nodded to her and shook Gabriel's hand, then glanced toward the stockade as the other womenfolk emerged.

Mother adjusted Libby on her hip, waved, and called out. "Come inside and let us refresh you."

"I must be speedy, Mrs. White, for a small party of Loyalists be on my tail."

She placed a hand on her heart. "What shall we do?"

"I suggest you repair posthaste to Fort Martin, for the few behind me are of the least concern." Caylan removed his cocked hat and smoothed the hair come loose from his queue, then met Jenny's wide eyes.

"Who?" she breathed.

"We hemmed some British in at Carr's and were about to fire the fort when General Pickens got word a troop of Loyalists passed through Ninety Six, headed for Georgia. They march under James Boyd, an Irishman from South Carolina commissioned to recruit in these parts. We tried to head them off on the Broad. They got across north of us and are now at the ferries there. Our men head for Clark's. Nail's men scouted north of the Broad, but Clark loosed me south of the river to ride ahead of the enemy and report their movements." Caylan bowed his head to their mother, who'd drawn closer as he spoke. "I had to warn you, I expect the entire British force to cross Long Creek before nightfall."

"Merciful heavens," Hester whispered. Caylan's hand shot out to steady her elbow when she swayed.

"West at John Hill's stockade, you should be safe. But you must make haste."

"There will be a battle." Gabriel clenched and unclenched his fists. "The armies are too close."

Caylan speared him with a sharp, perceptive glance. "Aye. I fear so."

He sucked in a breath. "Take me with you, Caylan. I can mount up in ten minutes."

"Gabriel," their mother moaned. Did she fear more for her son or his desertion of them in the face of danger?

Regardless, Jenny reached out and took the musket from her brother's hand. She glowered. "You know what Father said. We need your help getting away on time."

"I do not report to you," Gabriel snapped, squaring his still-slender shoulders. "Clark's son returns from North Carolina to fight by his father. With battle brewing mere miles from our land, would Father not have me do likewise?"

Caylan took in the cringing stances of Jenny's mother and sister before he replied. "You should do your duty as your father last outlined, lad. I spoke to him before riding out, and while he asked me to send you to Hill's, he spoke naught of your enlistment."

Gabriel's beardless jaw tightened.

"Go prepare the livestock," Jenny told him, returning the musket. He promptly shouldered it and stalked off. Mother hurried after him. Jenny's fingers twined in the reins of Caylan's stallion. "We must show your horse to ford Dry Fork and continue south, but circle back into the creek and hide in the swamp west of here 'til they have passed."

"Aye." As he took the leather, his fingers briefly encircled hers. "I will be close enough to come to your aid should there be trouble."

She looked away. He meant the touch to be reassuring, nothing more. What did it say that her fear of McIntosh facing a British scouting party alone frightened her more than diverting them herself? She blinked, focusing on the business at hand. "We shall deal with them. You should keep yourself concealed and complete your mission."

Hester cleared her throat. "And pray, what is my task, to pack?"

Caylan's gaze gentled as he looked at her. "Aye, lass. Hurry."

She gave him a longing look before scurrying away.

Jenny called after her, "Hester, should these scouts stop in, conceal your preparations and get in bed as though you are ill."

Wide-eyed, over-the-shoulder glance illustrating her alarm, Hester nodded. Her toe slipped on a patch of grass dampened by recent rain, and she almost fell before running into the stockade.

Caylan looked back at Jenny with a glow in his narrowed eyes. "Clever lass. Methinks we can count on you to keep them alive."

Fifteen minutes later, Jenny felt the absence of the Scot's presence like an ache in a molar when she returned to the fork. She hadn't time to trundle the barrow inside before three mounted men appeared on the Indian path. She grabbed the shovel and went back to work, pausing to act surprised as they splashed into the water.

"Ho! Woman!" called the ringleader, a stout, crusty man with greasy raven's hair, as he pulled up next to her. He wore the dress of the backcountry scout rather than a British regular.

Jenny's childhood pranks had included the practice of loosing one eye to roam on its own. Though making the face would more likely result in abuse than laughter in this instance, playact again, she must. And most convincingly. She gazed up at him with lack of focus and her lower lip hanging slightly slack. "*Ja?*"

"Has a man ridden this way recently?"

"I seen no man." She went back to smoothing manure right beside the intentional hoof prints of Caylan's horse.

A companion edged his mount closer. "Whaddya mean? Them is fresh tracks right there!" He pointed to the ground with his rifle butt, then poked her shoulder with it. "Where you hidin' him?"

As though startled, Jenny let loose her shovel, scattering cow dung over the man's boot and stirrup.

"You bracket-faced, stupid wench!" He hit her over the collarbone with his weapon.

Jenny's bellow of protest disintegrated into wailing loud enough to warn her mother and siblings. She fell to the ground and covered her head. "I seen no one, I seen no one!" she kept yelling as she thrashed about.

Out of the corner of her eye, she noticed the third man had followed the tracks. He edged his horse between Jenny and her offender. "Leave off, Little. The frau is clearly betwattled. See here, the rebel rode on south."

"Ja, he went thatta way!" Jenny cried and pointed without looking up.

A clod of flying spit deposited on her neck as a

calling card, the Loyalists thundered off. Jenny remained a minute with her head covered, heart thudding, thanking the Good Lord above for endowing her with ample acting skills. She could take the stage in Charleston, she could. Then, rubbing her collarbone, she sat up and looked around, laughing.

Her sister came flying out of the stockade sans cap, face the pastiest white Jenny had ever seen. "We saw them leave! Are you all right?"

"Yes." Jenny stood and brushed dirt off her petticoat.

"Will they come back?"

"Not until after we are gone." Jenny studied her sister, touching her arm. "Are you that frightened, little dove?"

"No, silly, Mother put flour on my face when you screamed. She said they would search the house, and I must look pox-stricken."

Laughing again, Jenny grabbed Hester's hand and ran. "It would seem you need me less than McIntosh thought." On the cabin porch, she asked, "Are you packed?"

"Yes, but Jenny?" Hester stopped and glanced toward the shed.

She tried not to sound as impatient as she felt. "What?"

"You have to tie the cows on the rope and take off their bells. I fear our brother has gone to the war."

*L*ike most frontier stockades, the walls of Fort Martin contained several small ramshackle cabins apart from the family abode. These now sheltered not just the Whites but women and children from several other area families.

After bringing her mother and younger sisters to relative safety, Jenny lay awake. From her place on the hard floor, she listened to the sounds of breathing and watched the shuttered window for signs of dawn. When faint pink lit the cracks, she slipped from the quilt next to Hester and made her way to the horse pen.

She found Merry's saddle in the barn and called the mare.

"Where are you going?"

About to mount, Jenny whirled. Wrapped in her cloak against the soft drizzle, Hester crossed her arms and frowned. Behind her, lights flickered in the Hill family cabin, and a wisp of smoke curled from the chimney.

"I...have a bad feeling. I cannot hide here and wait for news."

"What is the bad feeling?"

Jenny swung into the saddle. "I only aim to ride out a ways and scout. And if I can, to bring our brother back. I will be safe. I know these woods better than any man."

"Yes, but you are *not* a man. What would happen if the wrong rogue came upon you?"

Jenny lifted her chin. "I would like to see him try anything."

Hester shook her golden curls. "Yes, but you have no gun, Jenny."

Jenny patted the bow and quiver strapped to her back. "I should rejoin you here today or tomorrow."

As Hester launched herself forward, Jenny tapped the mare's sides with her heels. She could not stay to listen to her sister's fears, and she could not explain to Hester the intense pull she felt toward the south.

True, at first, she had been angry with Gabriel. But she could not blame him for going. They shared the same volatile blood, the same longing for freedom.

When the walls of Fort White appeared ahead, Jenny paused long enough to enjoy a moment of relief and investigate the stockade with caution. Provisions had been taken, cleavers strewn about on the floor from the torn-open mattress, the three-legged stool broken. Likely only the extreme haste of the invaders had spared their home the torch. Their livestock remained safe at Fort Martin, and their hiding place under the floor still concealed their medicinal herbs, precious seasonings, tools, and coin. She lifted out the wooden box of herbs she and her mother had dug and dried the previous season, placing it in her haversack.

Jenny set out following the Indian trail the Loyalists had taken the day before. Since the underbrush was cleared off with annual burnings and the canopy of forest above kept the drizzle off, the going was not rough despite the narrow path.

As she rode, she sorted the purpose of her mission. She did hope to bring Gabriel back. She considered him little more than a boy-child, yet something about a brother's presence transferred the invisible mantle of responsibility from her shoulders. With Gabriel gone, she was less "womanfolk" and more protector. Was she not already capable enough?

But there was more. She feared not only for Gabriel, but for Caylan. She doubted not the Highlander could care for himself. But men died in battle. And the thought of him dead was like to a panther's claws having sundered her chest. Was she really so needy that the passing attention of a kind man enlisted her immediate devotion?

Jenny came to what had been a campsite where another large host had crossed the same ground more recently. The Patriots.

A distant din lifted on the morning air. She paused,

listening. Yes, drums and muskets. Capping her canteen, she spurred Merry on, sick to her stomach. The thunder of battle grew louder for a time, but about noon, silence descended, while thick smoke hovered.

With sounds of her approach no longer covered by the noise of the fray near Kettle Creek, Jenny slowed her pace. Of a sudden, cardinal-red flashed through the trees. She dismounted and hid herself...until she ascertained the wearer of the cloth lay fixed against a tree. Wounded? Dead? Looping Merry's reins around a sapling, she approached Indian-like until it became clear the regular in white and crimson had expired. Thanking God for His marvelous provision, Jenny lay claim to his Brown Bess and necessary accoutrements.

As she led her mare forward, the trail that wound to a cattle pen atop a hill in a bend in the creek became increasingly littered with men—wounded, dead, and prisoners in small groups herded by soldiers in buff and blue. "What has happened here?" she asked the first Continental line officer she saw.

"A great victory for the Patriots, ma'am, and a clear message to King George III he shall not raise troops from Georgia."

Jenny let out a breath in relief. "And our wounded?" She held down Merry's head as the horse snorted, disturbed by the smell of blood. She tried not to study a

British officer a stone's throw from them, his face blown away by a musket ball.

"Still scattered on the battlefield."

"Where did Colonel Clark fight?"

"Pickens spearheaded the main battle here, when we caught Boyd's men parching corn and slaughtering cattle. He tried to hold the fence row but fell in the retreat. In fact, the colonel was just there, tending the rogue's dying requests. Dooly and Clark flanked the enemy, bursting from the swamp on the other side of the hill just as the lobster backs re-formed across the creek." He pointed.

"Have the colonels and their regiments quit the area?"

"Yes, ma'am, marching on toward Savannah."

Then all that was left was to scan the wounded. Thanking the officer with scarce a look at the contingent of sullen and bedraggled prisoners, Jenny hurried away. Heart in her throat, calling out for her father, brother, and Caylan, she visited each fallen man. The wounded begged for aid. She paused only long enough to offer a word of comfort and a sip from her canteen. She thought of the herb box in her possession but could not spare the time to employ its contents. Not until she knew if those she sought lay crumpled in the tangled bog near Kettle Creek.

In a trampled patch of rivercane, an English soldier

sprawled face down in the mud. His blood splattered the remaining stalks. On the other side of an oak tree, in a man's inert grasp, lay a rare beauty of a Kentucky rifle—one she had last seen gleaming by the firelight of their cabin. With a cry, she rounded the inlet.

"Caylan!" She knelt beside the scout and slid a hand under his neck.

His eyes sprang open, and he fumbled to raise his weapon.

Jenny's free hand shot up. "No, no, 'tis me, Jenny White!"

"Zounds, woman, I could have killed you! What are ye doing here?" He let the rifle fall back beside him. His jaw, sorely in need of a razor, clamped tight, while perspiration sprang out on his forehead despite the damp February chill.

"Looking for my father and brother. Gabriel followed you, you know."

"I know. I tried to send him back." Caylan struggled to a sitting position but grimaced and paused on his elbows.

Jenny's lips parted as fresh blood oozed onto his legging below his fringed shirt. "That looks bad."

"The ball's still in there."

Reaching in her haversack, Jenny flicked out a long knife.

"Whoa!" Caylan yelled.

She bit back a grin. "The ball will have to wait," she said as she nipped the linen haversack strap at both ends. "But I do have an ointment that should help staunch the bleeding."

She tugged on the damp rip of Caylan's leggings until the fabric parted a bit more, causing him to grunt. As Jenny opened the herb box and removed a small pot, Caylan craned to watch. She raised her skirt to cut off a length of her linen shift, making a thick pad of the material. After dabbing his wound, she paused with a glob of ointment on her finger.

"What's in that?" he asked with some suspicion.

"Yarrow."

"My people make such an ointment, but how did ye come to know of it?"

"Can you raise your leg up a bit?" As he complied, she smeared the medicine onto the pad, then used it to cover the gaping hole in his flesh. Lower lip between her teeth, Jenny secured the material with half of the haversack strap before glancing up. "I have a way with herbs, and I ask everyone I meet of their herb lore."

Caylan hung his head back and closed his eyes. Through stiff lips, he muttered, "Your father and Gabriel are fine. With Clark."

"Thank God. So I suppose the sense of urgency I had was for you."

Confusion clouded Caylan's brown eyes. "For me, lass? What do ye mean?"

Jenny gave her head a dismissive shake. "I did not understand it. I just felt I had to come. I thought I was to bring Gabriel home—alive, wounded, or dead—but I think God put it in my head to follow the armies here to aid you. I will bring you back to our place."

"Why would God send you to me?"

"Do you not believe in Him?" Jenny tied the knot and looked into her companion's eyes.

"Yes." The word hissed out between his teeth. "'Tis for His freedom that I fight."

Jenny nodded. "Then 'tis why. Come, lean on your rifle. Try to stand. I must get you on my mare."

As she placed an arm under Caylan's shoulders and moved toward Merry, he muttered in her ear, "'Tis possible He did send you, and with a sense of humor."

"What do you mean?"

"Do you know what today is?"

Jenny shook her head.

"St. Valentine's. The first person ye see of the opposite sex on this day is destined to be yer spouse." His breath stirred her hair in a laugh.

But she had the sense he was not laughing *at* her. Her confusion over that caused her tone to be all the more defensive when she retorted, "Well, you are hardly the first man I have seen today, so to the devil with your Scottish fables."

"Yes, but ye are definitely the first woman I have seen. And ever by far the most remarkable."

Jenny was left to ponder those words long after Caylan passed out and she cradled the slumping weight of him on the ride home.

CHAPTER 4

*D*ark had fallen by the time they reached
Dry Fork Creek. Despite her cloak, Jenny's
face stung from the cold mist, her chapped hands stiffened on the reins, and her arms ached from holding
Caylan on the horse. No chance was she continuing to
Fort Martin. She rode into the eerie silence of her
family's stockade. Halting Merry right in front of the
cabin's porch, she dismounted and tugged until the
Highlander slid off with a groan. She barely
caught him.

"Lieutenant McIntosh." Jenny lightly slapped at the
whiskering face. "You must hold yourself up. I may be
strong, but I cannot carry a gilly gaupus such as
yourself."

"Now ye use my own people's words against me.

Why should I wish to enter a house with a woman so set on giving me a good chivy?"

"Because if we do not get that lead shot out, you will surely die."

"Huzzah. More torture ahead." But Caylan shuffled over the threshold, leaning heavily on Jenny.

In the dark, she led him by memory. She was barely able to one-handedly toss the ruined mattress on her parents' bedstead before the lieutenant collapsed on it. His feet hung over the end.

"I will return posthaste once I see to the horse."

Having unsaddled, fed, and watered the horse, Jenny fetched water from the creek. She bolted the stockade gate and carried the pack burdens to the cabin. Caylan's labored breathing rasped loudly as she felt in the inky blackness for the tinder box. Adding kindling to the grate, she reached for the flint. It took a number of tries, but finally, welcome orange light illuminated the room. Jenny sat back with a sigh to find Caylan watching her.

Jenny fed the fire, then brought her canteen to the bed. She helped him sip and settled his head on Mother's prized goose-down pillow. Lowering the canteen from her own drink, she froze. Caylan's entire leg was slick and dark. She released a shaky breath.

"Slide the oilcloth from my pack under my leg," Caylan said.

Jenny did so, then told him, "I will boil water."

"Use the whiskey in my haversack. Pour it on that knife of yours and on the wound."

Jenny bristled. "I know what to do."

"Well, ye dinna know about the whiskey, now did ye?"

She placed a hand on her hip. "I might have guessed."

The disheveled head raised in protest. "I never drink to get drunk, lass, just to avoid the galloping sickness when clean water's not to be had. Much like yer cider."

She firmed her lips at the mention of galloping sickness and turned to her task.

"Hey, hand me the flask. Under the circumstances, getting a wee bit rammaged is in order."

"Well, in this case, I agree." Jenny put the silver container into Caylan's hand.

She built up the fire, hung a cauldron of water over the flames, and screwed a precious beeswax candle into the holder beside the bed. Minutes later, she perched next to her patient with clean rags, tongs, and the knife. Caylan bit his lip as Jenny removed his moccasins, then he reached under his shirt to untie the woven garter holding up the sodden legging. Gingerly, she peeled it off and dropped it on the floor. A trickle of blood ran from under the useless bandage and dripped on the oilcloth.

Breathing shallow, she raised her eyes to his.

He nodded. "Ye can do it, lass."

Jenny swallowed hard, removed the pad, and dabbed the wound with a rag.

"The bullet went straight in. I think it lodged against the bone. Lucky it must not have hit a major channel, or I would have bled out by now."

"Dutch comfort." Jenny splashed the round wound with alcohol and reached for the knife. Holding her breath, she leaned around to avoid creating a shadow and inserted the knife to hold the flesh back. She puffed out a quick sentence. "I don't see anything."

Body stiff as a poker, Caylan spoke through gritted teeth. "Then ye're gonna have to fish for it, lass."

The next few minutes were the worst of Jenny's life, and, she imagined, Caylan's too. How he did not pass out or even scream boggled her senses. By the time the small metal ball chinked into the tin cup on the bedside table, the lieutenant lay as limp as a fought-out fish on a bank. She splashed more whiskey on the wound, which roused him with a stifled curse, then applied another yarrow bandage.

Breathing hard, Jenny staggered to the porch, where she washed her blood-soaked hands and leaned on the post to steady her stomach and heart. She drank in lungfuls of the cold, woodsmoke-scented air.

Finally composed, she returned to the cabin to slide

more whiskey and water between Caylan's parched lips and gently wash his leg and hands with the boiled water and lye soap. At last, she pulled Mother's quilt from its hiding place under the floorboard and spread it over his recumbent form. Jenny rose to make her way to the loft when a hand snaked out and took hers.

"Stay," Caylan whispered. His eyes glowed molten in the firelight. "Lie beside me. Please."

Jenny's heart shot to her throat and lodged there, making her unable to speak. She shook her head. "'Twould be unseemly."

His lips turned down. "Tell me how I am to take advantage of you in this state."

That such a notion would even cross his mind made her work to find an answer. "Still, 'tis not right."

"Who will know?"

"That is not the point."

"What are you so afraid of?"

Standing silent, she felt sick.

He dropped her hand, turned his face toward the wall. "Go, then."

She could never resist a challenge, and challenge this was, for all its camouflage. Jenny toed off her shoes, lifted the quilt, and slid in beside him. The space was so limited she had to face him. She tried to tuck her arms at her sides, but Caylan caught her hand and pulled it up to his chest, clasped in his. She looked up, breath catching.

He smiled down at her. "Ye did good, lass." His fingers chafed hers a minute, then he fell asleep, his deepened breathing accompanied by the popping of the fire.

Exhausted as she was, Jenny lay frozen in wonder. His heart beat beneath her fingertips, not strong, but strong enough. She inhaled his scent—sweat, smoke, leather, and spice. She studied the dark-brown hair fanned out on her mother's pillow and the shadows on Scottish cheekbones and nose. The stubble on the square jaw. The softness of lips in repose. She shuddered with longing. She had better soak in this moment because it wasn't likely to ever come again.

---

*J*enny woke with the dawn, startled and guilty to find her head cradled on Caylan's chest. She stole from the bed to the fireplace to stir up the coals and boil water. The lieutenant's blood-darkened bandage sent her to the creek beds in search of fresh yarrow or plantain leaves. While she was out, she washed as best she could. Her hair felt heavy, greasy. Since her guest still slept upon her return to the cabin, she left a medicinal tea steeping while she allowed herself a quick hair washing.

The warm water on her scalp felt wonderful. By the fire, she dried and combed the long red locks. Her one beauty. Well, that and her name. Did Caylan like her hair?

The Whites did not own a looking glass, and Jenny avoided them in stores and other people's homes. The Loyalist had called her "bracket-faced." While she did not consider herself harsh featured, her bone structure was strong, and a smattering of freckles kissed her nose. But Gabriel said he could always tell when Jenny was up to something by the light of mischief in her eyes, and Hester said Jenny's smile stopped the sun. So it must not be all bad. Mostly, she wished for a dainty form like Hester's. Her height and build made her feel like a mannish oaf, devoid of grace. But last night, lying next to Caylan, for the first time, she had felt like a sparrow nestled in a crevice of the rock.

What was this sudden preoccupation with her appearance? Jenny drew in her lips, shoving the comb into one of her shift pockets and going to start the morning mush.

When Caylan called her name, Jenny froze. It had the sound of a North Carolina mountain brook. Beautiful, indeed. So startling, she jerked around and frowned at him.

"Who gave you leave to call me that?"

"'Tis yer name, is it not?"

"Not the one you should be using."

Caylan pulled himself up on his elbows. "Well, no need to get uppish, *Miss* White. I just thought having a lass dig a bullet out of a man's leg, then passing the night side by side, might entitle the pair to the use of Christian names."

He made a fair point. She stood there gnawing her lower lip.

Caylan gestured her closer. "Can ye look at me leg? 'Tis paining me something fierce."

"Of course." Jenny gathered boiled water and fresh linens and hurried over, contrite. What right had she to sass a wounded soldier? Surely, his sacrifice granted him an extra measure of grace. "I brought plantain leaves to make a poultice and prepared a tea."

"And washed yer hair." Caylan's tone softened as he grasped a strand between his thumb and forefinger, letting it trail through his grasp. She froze in the act of untying the old wrapping. His wistful gaze dissolved in a blink. "Sorry. I don't need you venting your spleen again."

Jenny glanced down. "I won't. And you may call me by my given name, at least when we are alone." To distract both of them as she applied the poultice, she asked, "Will you tell me of my father and brother in the battle? Did Gabriel acquit himself well?"

"Aye, lass. We tied our mounts before the battle—"

Her hands stilled in horror. "Did we leave your horse at Kettle Creek?"

He grinned. "Nae, some other well-bodied Patriot rides him now. I know the man, and he will return him if both survive."

"You think they go straight to another encounter."

"I think it unavoidable."

Jenny shuddered.

"Your brother will be fine. At least, he has as much chance as any of them. I did not see much of him along that cane-choked creek, but I know he shot at least two of the enemy. He is as much frontiersman as any. And a boy of almost fifteen is considered a man, ye know."

She sighed, bathing Caylan's now-bandaged leg. "I know. I think it is just extra hard because we lost our younger brother shortly after we moved here."

Caylan cocked his head. "Ye did?"

"Yes. To rattlesnake bite. Increase was only nine."

"'Tis a hard land. Lachlan McIntosh lost his younger brother, Lewis, shortly after he came to Georgia, too...to an alligator during a swim in the creek." As Jenny's widened eyes met his while she offered the tin cup, Caylan nodded. He cradled the tea and continued. "All men die, 'tis just a matter of when, and how bravely.

Let it be said of me when I go that I went down fighting. Your brother and father are of the same mind, lass. 'Tis why we are such friends. At least we have the comfort of knowing where our family members go when that moment comes."

Jenny merely nodded. This was not the proper moment to engage him in a debate over Separatist Baptist free will versus Presbyterian predestination.

Caylan dipped his head to take a sip. Jenny was resisting the powerful urge to smooth back his loose hair when he spit and yelled. "For mercy's sake, woman, what did ye put in this brew?"

"Elderberry and yellow dock. To strengthen the blood and ward off possible distemper." Jenny laughed. "Now, be a brave Highlander and drink it all down. You must rest."

"Agreed, although..." He paused to down the tea, his face twisting into a fierce grimace, then clunked the cup onto the bedside table. "I feel powerful in need of a good scrubbing myself." He ran his hand over his jaw.

"Later. Raise your head up a minute."

Caylan eyed her with suspicion but did as she requested. Jenny slipped the wooden comb from her pocket, slid the half-entangled twine from Caylan's mahogany locks, and ran the tines through them. She tried to think as if she was doing Libby's hair, efficient and quick, but it was not like that at all. It felt far more personal than she had expected. He looked handsome and vulnerable with his hair about his strong features. When she finished, she helped him ease back onto the pillow.

"Caylan?" She froze. She had just spoken his given name completely without intention.

He made no comment, but his gaze was tender as it lit on her. "Aye, lass?"

How could one little word make her feel as dainty as Hester? She swallowed. "If the armies go to the coast now, do you think it safe for me to fetch my mother and sisters home?"

"I do."

"Will you be comfortable if I go?"

"Dinna worry about me. I shall probably still be sleeping when ye return."

Jenny nodded. "Then I shall prop your gun by your bed and ride out posthaste."

His eyelids drifted shut. "Thank ye, Jenny, for taking such good care of me."

Her heart warmed. She rose, but she stood there watching him sleep. She did not want to go get her family, most especially her lovely sister. She wanted to linger in this cabin alone with Caylan McIntosh, pretending what would never be.

CHAPTER 5

*J*enny clattered the dishes as she cleared the board, then seized the broom. Maybe if she ignored Caylan's scout friend who'd arrived today from Nail's troop, he would go away. He told them Lieutenant Colonel Prevost had routed the Americans at Brier Creek near Savannah, returning the lower part of the state to British rule. And worse, hundreds of Indians under a Colonel Taitt had laid siege to hapless settlers.

Evidence of the native uprising arrived only minutes ago, a sixteen-year-old boy and his grandmother from the tail of Dry Fork, burned out by the Indians. They now occupied a small cabin in the enclosure. The resultant call to arms for all Wilkes Patriots over the age of sixteen meant Caylan would be leaving with this wiry hatchet man, John Dunn. So would the youth, judging from his murmured conversations with the soldiers. They would rally across the border in South Carolina.

So now not only must she worry over her father and Gabriel, but Caylan as well.

He was not even healed yet, though he had said to her just yesterday, "I need to go back, Jenny. If I can cross-cut your land, I can sit a horse."

The fact that she would worry for him stung like a hornet. It helped not that the man sat over there now oiling his rifle, his splayed leg almost touching Hester's skirt. Jenny was also out of temper with Hester, who dropped in seeds while Jenny made furrows and sat with piecework in her lap while Jenny cleaned up after dinner. Jenny's back hurt so bad from planting in the new ground Father had cleared by girdling trees and uprooting their stumps before he left that she scarce could swing the broom. Meanwhile, Hester hummed a soft tune to accompany the men's military preparations.

"What is that, Miss White? 'Johnny Has Gone for a Soldier'?" Dunn's glittering dark eyes fixed on her.

"'Tis, indeed."

"You have a nice voice. Would you sing it for us?"

Hester pressed her full lips together, containing a smile. "I fear singing would slow me, Mr. Dunn, and I must finish this last shirt."

"'Tis good of ye to make more than one shirt each for yer father and brother, lass," Caylan commented, glancing at Hester's quick, fair hands.

"Why, this shirt is not for them, Lieutenant McIntosh, but for you."

Jenny's broom ceased its motion.

"For me?" Surprise colored Caylan's voice.

"Yes. I could not help but notice how threadbare yours is." Hester's fair brows drew together, and her gaze sought the corner bed, where their mother rose from tucking Libby in. "'Twas not improper given the circumstances, was it, Mother?"

"I think it good-hearted," Mother said, taking a seat next to her middle daughter. "And I also think it would be kind to oblige Mr. Dunn's request. Then 'tis my fondest hope Lieutenant McIntosh will read to us from my husband's Bible. I fear this may be the last occasion for a while."

"'Twould be my pleasure, ma'am." Caylan turned to Hester. "And I thank you for your generous gift."

When her sister rendered her tune, Jenny took the ashes out to the hopper, but the sweet notes followed her into the cool March night.

Here I sit on Buttermilk Hill
Who can blame me, cryin' my fill
And ev'ry tear would turn a mill
Johnny has gone for a soldier

Jenny clasped her arms around herself as the haunting melody swirled around her, making her want to dissolve into unexpected sobs. What was wrong with her? She must get hold of herself. At a movement from the smaller cabin, Jenny straightened. The boy stood on the porch, watching her.

When Jenny went back in, her mother suggested, "Let us hear from the Psalms tonight."

Jenny lowered herself onto a bench while her mother placed the priceless Bible from England on Caylan's lap. She expected to hear of God keeping one from the arrow by day and the pestilence by night, or Him being a shield and strong tower, but Caylan read from Psalm 139.

"'Whither shall I go from thy spirit? Or whither shall I flee from thy presence?'"

Hearing the passage in the man's deep Scottish lilt made Libby fall asleep in her mother's bed, sucking her thumb, and Jenny's heart flip over.

"'Thou hast covered me in my mother's womb. I will praise thee; for I am fearfully and wonderfully made: marvelous are thy works; and that my soul knoweth right well. My substance was not hid from thee, when I was made in secret, and curiously wrought in the lowest parts of the earth. Thine eyes did see my substance, yet being unperfect; and in thy book all my members were written, which in continuance were fashioned, when as yet there was none of them.'"

Jenny shifted on the bench, taking pressure off her sore thighs. She glared at him. Had he chosen this passage on purpose? To goad her?

Finally, he concluded, "'See if there be any wicked way in me, and lead me in the way everlasting.'"

"Amen," said her mother.

Even Dunn bowed his head a moment.

"Thank you, Lieutenant," Hester whispered. The look she turned upon him was almost worshipful.

"My pleasure, Miss White." Caylan closed the book, returning it to Jenny's mother.

How fitting Caylan and Hester looked together. Why would everyone insist on wedding vows had Hester spent the night alone with the wounded man, but when Jenny did, all she earned was a look of concern? Or had it been pity?

Before Jenny could puzzle that out, Hester sat up straight, holding up the material in her lap. "There, I believe the shirt 'tis done. Would you try it on, Lieutenant?"

Jenny got up. "Excuse me. I shall see to the livestock for the night."

After a few minutes of shoveling hay to the horses in the barn, a long shadow fell over her. She whirled to behold Caylan. In his new shirt. She pressed her lips together and continued her task.

"Soon the livestock can be turned out on the greening grass, the pea vines, and the wild oats." Limping slightly, Caylan moved around her and took the pitchfork out of her hand. "Rest. Ye have done enough today."

"And you have not?"

"Can ye never accept an offer of help?"

"Thank you. I shall milk the cow." Jenny turned to fetch a bucket, but Caylan dropped the tool and caught her hand.

"Why are ye out of temper with me, lass?"

"I am not."

"Yes, ye are. Is it because I am leaving? Ye know I have to go."

Jenny pulled her hand away. "Of course. I *want* you to go."

A frown flitted over his forehead. "And why is that?"

She tilted up her chin as she backed from him. "To fight for our freedom, naturally."

"And is that all?" His voice lowered to a rumble, stopping her at the stable door. "'Twouldn't have anything to do with your sister?"

Why did he insist on speaking what should not be spoken, what she thought remained hidden? "Why should she have bearing on aught?"

"Because her differences from ye stick in yer craw, and make ye think yer own attributes lacking."

Jenny's gaze swung to his, hot and accusing. "You *did* read that passage on purpose."

"I wanted ye to hear how the Creator views ye."

"'Curiously wrought.' Yes, I caught that part."

"Is that what ye think of yerself?"

"I know what I am, and I know what I am not. And I fail to see how it is any of your concern."

"Then I will tell you. Did ye know the Scots women of New Inverness held property? Were trained in the Manual of Arms? Served the cannon of Fort Darien when the men left to fight the Spanish?"

She shook her head. The intensity in Caylan's voice had made her throat tighten. Whatever point he was coming to, he felt it deeply. And so would she. Jenny swallowed.

He nodded. "'Twas the heritage of my own grandmother, and a proud one. When I look at ye, Jenny White, I see her. The kind of woman bred to life on a frontier. The kind who not only survives, but thrives. Aye, yer sister is lovely, but she was not the one who stood her ground before savages, or fed her family through the winter. Or got this wounded lout on a horse, fished a bullet out of his leg, and cured him with herbs. *Ye* did that, Jenny White. It's ye who stirs my blood. So yes, I am leaving tomorrow. But rest assured, I will be back."

She was already breathless before he started toward her. In two long strides, Caylan took her in his arms. Jenny's world spun when he claimed her mouth with his. Her first kiss. It melted her, seared her, like butter in a hot skillet. Immersed her, like the sun-drenched creek water on a fine summer's day, cleansed her sore-aching aloneness with a flood of being desired and desire. She grasped his strong shoulder blades through Hester's shirt as his fingers tangled in her hair and drank in the essence of the man she knew in that instant she loved.

"Sweet heavens, lass." Caylan pulled back long enough to stare at her in wonder and run a thumb over her bottom lip.

She'd behaved like a hussy. All but pushed him into the hay. "I—I'm sorry—"

"Don't ye dare apologize, for it took that kiss to tell me what you would not." He cradled her jaw, but she evaded his gaze, keeping her lashes lowered. "Jenny, did ye think what passed between us after the battle meant nothing?"

"You were a wounded man in need of comfort, and you had drank more than a little whiskey." She swallowed hard. "I set no special stock by it." What a clanker.

A chuckle rumbled in his chest, hinting that she

hadn't fooled him for a moment. "Well, I knew from that night when I held ye in my arms, rammaged as I was, that ye were the only one I ever wanted there again. Do ye believe it now?"

No. She did not believe it. She was living a wild dream that she would soon wake from.

A dove cooed just outside the fort wall. Caylan cocked his head.

"'Tis only a mourning dove," Jenny whispered. Despite her best intentions, she trembled with longing. She wanted to touch him, run her hand over his hair, his jaw, but she daren't.

His expression hardened, filling her with fear. "Nae. 'Tis not."

Before she could react, he had her by the hand, running to the cabin. She stumbled up the porch steps behind him. He burst through the front door with speed and, for such a large man, amazing stealth.

Everyone inside leapt to their feet.

"Indians," Caylan hissed. "Arm yourselves."

A night attack. Almost unheard of.

An Indian scaled the fort wall and tomahawked the neighbor boy on his porch before the Whites and their guests gathered their weapons. The wails of the grandmother drew the militia men out. Caylan's gun fired, dispatching the native in the yard, while John picked off another just clearing the stockade. The men ran to the loopholes, Jenny and her mother taking the other two. Mother carried Caylan's sawed-off Bess meant to be used from horseback.

The full moon would have provided just enough light for the Creeks to slip into the fort to murder the settlers, but the settlers struggled to distinguish their foes from the shadows in the woods. The Indians fired pitch arrows into the enclosure. Hester ran with wet burlap to beat the flames. More and more arrows sailed in with effect while more and more lead shot zinged out without any. Hester's cries grew frantic. Mother, then Jenny, abandoned their posts to assist. Another two natives tossed grappling hook and line up the wall, but Caylan's and John's expert marksmanship dropped the men in the clearing.

For a few more minutes, the women beat flames and the scouts rammed and fired. When Jenny ran to the wall, Caylan told her, "I think they are gone, but we should watch 'til dawn."

"I will resume my post." Her gaze fell on the elderly woman, weeping in the yard as her grandson took his last breaths. "The tree's carving did not stay them."

"What would have happened had John and I not been here?" Caylan's brows slashed deep over his eyes.

"They will come back. And next time, ye shall have no militia to guard yer walls."

"Other settlers will come now, hearing of the attacks."

"Women and children," Caylan spat, turning his head to scan the trees. A smear of black powder darkened his jawline. "Ye must convince yer mother to go. She will if ye suggest it."

"Go where, Caylan? We have no relatives, no town."

"Better a refugee camp than having yer home burnt down around you. I dinna want to return to that, Jenny."

The anger in his voice pushed her away. She sat at her loophole until dawn and John's investigation confirmed the party of warriors had retreated. Caylan was still cold, distant, as he packed and saddled the dead boy's horse. She brought him yeastless biscuits, jerky, dried fruit and nuts, little enough for the miles ahead. She did not care that her family watched, she only wanted him to take her in his arms as he had the night before. Kiss away her fears and anguish.

Having secured his pack, he turned to her. "Come with me."

"I cannot."

His jaw worked, and he looked away.

"Please, I cannot bear your anger." Jenny touched

his arm. "The protection of the tree may have failed, but God's has not."

"Ye're a foolhardy woman, and I can see ye're going to be the death of me." He reached down to unpin the McIntosh brooch from his shirt. Stepping up to her, he secured it on her bodice. His eyes bored into hers. "Be here when I come back for ye."

CHAPTER 6

*F*or about a week after Caylan gave Jenny his brooch, Hester made herself scarce. Finally, long lashes swept down, she haltingly expressed her pleasure that the lieutenant loved Jenny.

"He did not say he loved me," Jenny corrected her. But then, neither had she spoken those words. Their courtship had been too rushed, too unconventional.

"The feeling between you 'tis clear." Hester shook her head. "I want you to know, I can see why he admires you. You are much alike, you two. And I envy you. Whatever happens, at least you will have known love."

Jenny did not doubt what she felt, but neither could she hold Caylan to a pledge he had not made. With the war on, many months would pass before their paths were likely to cross again—each one subtly eroding whatever he'd thought he felt for her. She would not be one of those pitiful, pining women. She turned her attention to what lay before her as spring ripened into summer—nurturing the wheat, corn, vegetables, and flax, that plant so vital to the production of clothing.

Almost before they knew it, harvest was upon them —still with no sign of their men. A traveling peddler finally brought news that the Wilkes County militia had recruited more men to rally in South Carolina, preparing for another attempt to retake Savannah as the weather cooled. Meanwhile, other members of the militia remained in the backcountry to quell the threat of Creeks and Loyalists.

Each day before they went out to work the fields, and again before they locked the gates in the evenings, Jenny scouted the land around the fort for signs of intruders. Despite her vigilance, on a day it turned cold enough for making soap in the yard, Liberty squealed from her blanket and pointed at the fort wall behind Jenny. A quick glance nearly stopped Jenny's heart, for a brown eye peered through a low knothole.

Her arms reacted almost of their own accord. Lightning quick, she flung hot lye from the cauldron at the peeper. The resulting howl of pain confirmed her accuracy, and she called to Hester to watch Liberty while she grabbed a rope and hurried to hog-tie the man flailing about outside.

The capture of the spying Loyalist gave her an excuse to visit Hannah Harrington Clark at Fort Clark, where Jenny turned the man over to the militia. Her heart sank when her scan of the men inside the stockade failed to produce her father, brother, or Caylan. But she sat down to the small consolation of tea and sweet potato pie with the colonel's wife, whose similarly substantial frame and decisive nature always put her at ease.

As she'd hoped, Hannah possessed the latest political news. Colonel Dooly had dealt a measure of peace to Wilkes County that summer and fall of 1779, staying the Creeks at Gunnell's Fort and condemning seven Tories to death. She told of government wranglings in Augusta, the robbery and murder of Captain Robert Carr, and the capture of their neighbor, Patriot leader Stephen Heard.

After sharing all the news of the war she knew, Hannah regaled her with tales. It seemed she had made a dozen frilled-bosom shirts for Elijah the winter past, only to have one of her maids reveal their smokehouse hiding spot to a British raider. She also related the amazing release of Stephen Heard, whose slaves, Daddy Jack and Mammy Kate, rode to Augusta to rescue him from jail. Taking in fresh clothing, six-foot Kate carried the small-statured officer out on her head, concealed in the hamper of dirty linens.

On the ride back from Fort Clark, Jenny basked in the red sourwoods, the birdsong, the earthy scent of decaying leaves, and the camaraderie she'd experienced with another strong, courageous woman. A woman who had found deep love. Hope for her future stirred again.

Hester ran out of their cabin before Jenny dismounted Merry. "Oh, sister, come. Mother is feverish, casting up her accounts, a rash on her face, hands, and feet. Methinks 'tis the pox!"

So quickly, everything could change.

Jenny removed her sisters to the small cabin and tended her mother with warm herbal sponge baths, yarrow tea, drinking water exposed to tar, and as much circulating air as possible. But as her mother's body covered with the fearful bumps, then pustules, the risk remained huge. Since Liberty's birth, Mother had been weak. Now her body seemed not to have the resources to fight off the invader.

Hester left daily food offerings on the porch and stood in the yard to receive updates.

At the beginning of the third week, Jenny leaned on the doorframe and said through choking tears, "Pray."

By the end of the week, she found a spot in view of the stockade but well away from water sources to dig her mother's burial plot. After placing the slight burden in the ground, Jenny tossed the dirt back in while Hester and Libby sobbed a few feet away.

Jenny sank down to rest. The earth spun, and sweat sprang out under her shift despite the sharp November air. An invisible vise gripped her head. Without Father, Gabriel, and now Mother, the burden on her felt impossible to bear. What a blow this would be to Father and Gabriel.

"Since you've already given the house a good scrubbing, we can move back in. I'll go get our things," Hester said and started to turn, Libby's hand in hers.

Jenny gasped as she attempted to rise and her knees buckled. "I think not. For I believe I have contracted the pox." At Hester's look of horror, she added, "You and Liberty should go to the neighbors'." If they would take them in. She should have sent them farther away when Mother first fell ill.

Hester held a hand over her heart. "And abandon you? No, I must stay and nurse you, but I shall take Liberty away now."

"Hester, you may well contract the disease."

Hester squared her slight shoulders. "I am not such a selfish weakling I would leave my sister to die. I am in God's hands."

Over the next month, as Jenny instructed Hester in providing the same care she had rendered to their mother, she marveled at Hester's determination. She did all without complaint, taking little sleep or nourishment, sitting late into the night singing the hymns they had learned in the Yadkin Valley. Hester fought the darkness that tried to claim Jenny with equal strength to what Jenny had exhibited for their mother. But Hester won.

Her first day out of bed, her fingers shaking, Jenny traced the contour of pock marks left on her face by the pustules after the scabs fell off. Facing death would be easier than facing the man she loved with what little beauty she had possessed ravaged by an invader she could not intimidate or outwit.

MAY 1780

"*B*y Old Scratch's britches!" Turning the herb-seasoned trout with a spatula, Jenny jerked the pan off the fire and sat back on her haunches. Yes. She had not been mistaken. For that unmistakable brogue sounded again...and two other dear voices, booming over her sisters' cries of joy.

Jenny leapt to her feet and started to run out into the peach-tinted May twilight, then froze. She stepped away from the fire and waited.

A moment later, the door burst open and Hester ran

in, followed by three substantial forms in buckskin and linsey-woolsey. "Jenny, look who has come!"

Tears sprang to Jenny's eyes at the sight of her brother, dirty but looking near grown, and her father, holding Liberty with her arms clasped around his neck. She could not look at the Scotsman.

"There's my ginger-hackled Jenny," Father cried, wrapping her in an embrace. He smelled of gun powder and pine. "But where is my good wife?"

The shock of the men's appearance, relief at being held by her father, and the realization that he knew nothing of his wife's demise launched a triple assault on Jenny's normally firm senses. She started to sob, something she could not recall doing for perhaps ten years.

Her father pulled back with his eyes wide. "What is this?" As he swiped a tear from Jenny's cheek, his thumb dragged to a halt. "You have had the pox." He set Liberty on the floor and looked up toward the loft, then stumbled back to the doorway. "Elizabeth? Elizabeth!"

Jenny covered her face while Hester caught her father's hand and whispered, "Father, we lost her."

"Lord, help me, no! No!" Like a tree under an ax, their father fell to his knees on the porch. He bent his graying head under his arms and keened.

The sound made Jenny weep harder. Now of equal height, Gabriel embraced her.

Liberty stood by the table with a finger in her

mouth, staring with horrified fixation at Hester attempting to comfort their father. "Gabriel, pick her up, please," Hester said.

Wiping his own face, he did so, while Caylan stepped toward Jenny. "Have ye a hug for me, lass?" he asked gently.

When he held out his arms, Jenny flew into them. He would not want her now, but she did so need his comfort. He smoothed her back with long strokes and buried his face in her hair.

"'Tis sorry I am to hear about yer ma, Jenny. When did the plague strike?"

"November. I nursed her, then Hester nursed me."

"And ye managed on yer own since then, brave girl, but you are thin as a rail. Who knew 'twas not the Indians or the Tories I should have fretted about, but the pox."

When Caylan attempted to lift her face, Jenny jerked her chin away. "Pray, do not look at me."

"'Tis hardly noticeable."

He meant she was so bran-faced her freckles almost covered the scars. Jenny stepped away. "So you say in this light."

"Let him look at you and hold you, Jenny." Gabriel's eyes snapped over Liberty's curls. "He knows he could be like Father right now, unable to do either. Your bravery and goodness is all he has talked of for a year. Vanity 'tis not like you."

At her brother's rebuke, Jenny hung her head.

Caylan tipped her chin with his index finger. "Gabriel is right that ye musn't fear me. I am just so glad ye're alive."

Gabriel put his hand—man-sized now but still thin —on her arm. "I apologize, Jenny. 'Tis my grief talking."

Jenny managed a smile, wiped her face, and turned toward the fireplace. "Hester can take you and Father to Mother's grave. I shall finish supper."

As the others left the cabin, Caylan unloaded his gear, and Liberty's arm encircled Jenny's skirts. Understandably, the child had been clingy since the fall. Jenny lifted down the plates and utensils and bent to Liberty's level. "Can you set the board, Libby?"

The little girl nodded. With her sister occupied, Jenny stirred the mess of early potatoes and beans and cut the cornbread at the sideboard. "What brings you to these parts?" she asked over her shoulder. "I dare not hope 'tis an end to hostilities."

His moccasins scuffed closer. "Not by far. Did ye hear of the attempt to retake Savannah last fall?"

"We did." She shot him a glance as he settled at the bench, scooting back for Liberty to work around him. When he moved a lost fork beside a plate, Jenny resisted a smile. "A traveler around Christmas brought news that the French fleet came to our aid, and that one of the Patriot commanders demanded the British surrender the city."

"Aye, but they stalled until reinforcements arrived, so that when the Americans attempted to unseat them, they could not. Our dead and wounded was a thousand to a fraction of that for them."

Covering the cornbread, Jenny moaned. Such loss of life. When would it ever end?

When Caylan took a sip from his canteen, Jenny hurried to gather the pewter tankards. He continued while she placed them onto the end of the table. "Heard's Fort became the seat of government, while the enemy turned their eye on Charleston. The South Carolinians were weak from the pox themselves, Jenny, and could not hold their city either. It went bad for my relations at both sieges. At Charleston, they faced The Black Watch, fellow Highlanders with the Forty-second Regiment of Foot. It stung like gall for them to surrender. Dooly also surrendered the majority of his men at his fort, only to be—"

When Caylan suddenly stopped speaking, his brow lowering as he glanced at Liberty, Jenny shooed her toward the loft. "Why don't you go get those flowers you picked from your room, dear heart? They'd look beautiful on the table."

Her sister was all too eager to scamper up the ladder.

Caylan offered Jenny a grateful look and lowered his voice. "He was killed in his own bed, in front of his family, by six British regulars."

"Oh no!" Her own struggles forgotten, Jenny turned with one hand at her heart, the other clutching their pewter pitcher. "So that leaves Colonel Clark in charge of the Georgia militia?"

"Yes. He has furloughed his men for a few weeks to secure their farms, and hopes to rally those who signed the British oath of allegiance under duress."

"That is your job, then? To recruit?"

Caylan nodded. "I shall make forays into the back-country to gather information and men while your father and Gabriel set you on your feet."

Jenny's back, aching from plowing the cornfield and weeding the flax rows, sagged. "I shan't tell a clanker—a bit of assistance 'twould be handy. How long will you remain?"

"With the travel between here and the regiment, about a week. But Jenny?" He stood, frightfully close to her as she poured cider into the tankards.

"Yes?" Why must her voice sound so breathless, giving her feelings away?

He put a hand over the pitcher, forcing it to the table. "I have thought of ye every day, lass. Can ye give me reassurance 'tis been likewise for you...that things have not changed?"

She swallowed and focused on the wooden buttons of his vest. "I have thought of you, Caylan McIntosh, but things *have* changed."

Before he could insist on an explanation, steps sounded on the porch.

*C*aylan had been gone several days, Father and Gabriel prepared a far field, and Jenny stirred their clothes in a pot of boiling lye to rid them of "gentleman's invaders" when the same cardinal-red she recalled from Kettle Creek flashed through the trees on the far rise. Hot energy rushed through her veins. They were about to be visited by a British scouting party.

"Sweet Lord, help us," she whispered. And thought fast.

She fished the contents from her pot, deposited them in the half-filled ash hopper, and ran for the cabin. She arrested Hester in her bread making. "British coming! Quick, you must hide all of Father's and Gabriel's things beneath the floorboards."

Without waiting to see if her sister complied, Jenny darted back to her cauldron and dropped in the bedding. The boil resumed about the time the pounding sounded on the bolted fort door. Hiding or playing simple probably wouldn't pacify this time. She opened to the enemy, her expression somber. Four regulars rode into the stockade, their stallions encircling her.

"Do I address the mistress of this place?" the officer demanded.

"I am Jenny White, daughter of the owner."

"Lieutenant Bradley Adams. Is your father in residence?"

She wiped her hands on her apron. "He is not." Not at the moment, anyway.

"And where might he be?"

Jenny lifted her chin. "Why, he signed up to fight you British, sir." Hester would have kicked her.

The man's black beetle brows met while florid color stained his neck. "You are the one with the reputation for sass. I warn you, I shall have none of your brazen-faced ways."

Jenny clasped her hands behind her back in a show of vulnerability. "How might I be of service today?"

"We seek a recruiting party of Clark's militia, believed to be stopping here."

"You can see they are not."

"I see nothing as yet." With a hand flick, the lieutenant sent his privates to tie their horses and search the buildings. He dismounted and approached, hackles visibly rising when he had to look up at her. "You will prepare victuals and cider for the men."

Jenny glowered. His was just the sort of arrogance that roused her Patriot ire. "I will not aid and abet my enemy."

"You will, or suffer this fort burned down around your ears."

Fuming, she considered her options. With the men gone—thank God!—they were outgunned. She must appear to submit, at least for the moment. She led the oaf into the cabin and introduced her sister. To Hester's credit, she maintained her calm, and the room was free of masculine effects. She had even moved the trestle over the loose floorboard.

While the invaders searched the cabin, tossing the ticks about, riffling through anything closed, and causing Liberty to cry, Jenny and her sisters huddled together. Adams returned to the hearth, increasingly florid, just in time to receive the report that nothing outside yielded evidence of militia.

"I told you as much." The words leapt out of Jenny's mouth like a fox from the henhouse.

Adams whipped toward her, hate shining from his eyes. "Shut your bone box!"

The man's absolute disdain eroded whatever remained of her judgment. She wiped his spit from her cheek and glared back. "You think yourself so much smarter than us colonists, do you not? Yet I led the last passel of Loyalists to a false track while the man they sought hid in the swamp."

"Jenny!" Hester hissed.

His eyes narrowed. "And just where is this swamp?"

She suppressed a smirk, for the swamp lay in the opposite direction of the field her father and brother were clearing. "West of the fort, but you shall find no one there today."

"My men will ascertain that, and in the meantime, you shall cook that turkey caged in your yard."

"I will not!" That turkey was meant to feed their own family this night.

"You know what happened to Stephen Heard's wife and daughter."

She certainly did. The two had died in the snow after Tories evicted them. While the fair weather and nearby presence of the men ensured they would not meet a similar fate, neither did she want their home destroyed. Her stupid pride had snared her again. As she stared into the compassionless void behind Adams's pale green eyes, an idea formed.

"Sister, is there any corn liquor left over?"

"Why, yes, in the hidey-hole. But—"

"Fetch it, please, to ease the lieutenant's temper while we prepare the meal. Then join me in the yard to pluck the fowl."

Hester caught on. "Our apologies for seeming less than hospitable, Lieutenant. I am sure you understand the duress and fear we live under."

The man gave a sanctimonious nod and reached to unstrap his sabre. He lounged before the hearth while everyone did his bidding.

When Hester joined Jenny at the blood-stained chopping block, Jenny whispered, "When the men return empty-handed, we must keep the liquor flowing. Once they are foxed, I'll remove that chunk of chinking that's loose near the fireplace hidey-hole."

"But why?" Hester breathed the question out, her chest rising and falling rapidly.

"So I can try to get some of their muskets out of the cabin after I send you for water. Take Liberty with you. You know where we hid the conch shell at the fork tree. Father and Gabriel should come quickly. And forewarned."

Hester nodded.

As Jenny had hoped, the tired, grumpy men came in and leaned their muskets near the hearth. Soon the mouth-watering aroma of roasting turkey and vegetables filled the cabin. The strong spirits eased inhibitions, and the men laughed, talked, and flirted with Hester. When one patted Hester's behind, Jenny wanted to run him through with her knife. But with a great effort, she kept her mouth shut as she passed back and forth between the board and fireplace, where she removed the piece of chinking. When the soldiers broke into an off-key rendition of "Barbara Allen," Jenny sent her sisters for the water. She also began to slide the muskets one by one through the hole, out into the yard.

As she raised the third one, one of the privates yelled, "Hey! What're ya doin'?"

Jenny froze. Her heart hammered. She whirled around, the loaded gun trained on the startled company. "I am taking you captive in the name of the independent state of Georgia!" The blast of the conch shell glorified her announcement.

"Get her," the lieutenant shouted.

The three privates lunged. Jenny aimed at the closest man and pulled the trigger. A boom and a puff of smoke filled the cabin. The man dropped to the ground, gut shot, red gushing over his hand as his bulging eyes met Jenny's. Astonishment froze everyone for a split second before Jenny grabbed the other musket.

"My stars, she shot Martin," one of the men exclaimed.

Over the death gurgles of the wounded soldier, she yelled, "I will kill the next man who comes at me!"

"You dimwits, are you going to let a Patriot hussy be your undoing?" Adams waved toward Jenny. "Take her in hand!"

Should she shoot him? Take out the leader and be done with it? She aimed for the officer, but when his minions feinted in her direction, she swiveled the barrel back. Too many of them, one of her. As she had with the Loyalists tracking Caylan, she let her left eye slide to one side, causing the men to cry out and bluster in confusion.

"The wench's cross-eyed!"

"Whoa, honey! Take it easy."

"Who's she aiming at?"

As she allowed her musket to waver back and forth, they alternately ducked, hollered, craned their necks for a better view, and threw their hands up. It would've been hilarious if Jenny hadn't pictured any one of them jumping on her at any moment.

Finally, she'd had enough. "Sit down, all of you, with your hands on the board." She jerked a nod toward the table.

"Now, be reasonable, woman." Adams extended his hands, palms down. "You cannot hold four men at gunpoint indefinitely."

"No, but I can do so long enough for my sister to tie you, and my brother and father to come to our aid."

The lieutenant's realization that he'd been outmatched boiled up in a bellow. "I will *kill* you!" But he halted rather than following through on taking a step toward her when she fixated the weapon—and her level stare—on him again.

It took but five or ten minutes of maintaining a granite countenance to cover her roiling fear of a miscalculation, but seemed like an eternity, before not just Hester, Father, and Gabriel, but also Caylan—back, apparently, from Fort Martin—burst onto the scene.

"We heard shots," Hester gasped out. "Are you all right?"

Caylan took one look at Jenny fixing the musket on the British with jaw set before a grin broke over his rugged features. "Of course she is. She is War Woman."

CHAPTER 7

SEPTEMBER 1780

Flattened onto her belly with her Brown Bess laid across a fallen tree, Jenny tracked the progress of a squirrel storing nuts. Waiting until he perched in the crook of a limb, she prepared to pull the trigger when a rustle sounded behind her. Frowning, she swiveled her head but saw nothing unusual. She looked back. No squirrel. Growling a slang term her mother would have certainly protested, Jenny relaxed her stance. The next moment, someone tackled her from behind.

She spluttered, flipped over, and tried to raise her gun, but the attacker pinned her arms above her head, his weight pressing her struggling body down.

"Dinna scream. 'Tis me."

Jenny gasped as she looked into amber eyes alight with mischief. "What are you doing, Caylan McIntosh? I could have shot you!"

"I figured approaching ye from behind safer than the front."

His expression of adoration faded into regret as he perused her face. Jenny wanted to shrink into herself. Her scars would be fully visible up close, in the late-morning sunlight. But she could not get away before he lowered his head—his breath tickling her, making her dizzy—and pressed his lips to hers. Not in passion, but with a soft reverence. Respect. Pity? She could not get up fast enough, brushing dry leaves off her skirt.

"What are you doing here?" she asked breathlessly. "Are my father and Gabriel here too?"

Caylan came to a sitting position. "Just me, and despite my entrance, my mission is dire. Take me to yer sister so ye both can hear all."

"But I was about to get our supper."

"No time for that." Fetching his accoutrements from a nearby tree, Caylan held out his hand.

Jenny ignored him, taking up her gun and setting out. "We heard of the battle at Musgrove's Mill last month and knew you were nearby."

"Aye, lass, there have been several battles since I saw

ye last." Sadness tinged Caylan's tone. "Elijah and his son were both wounded, Clark almost taken prisoner."

Jenny nodded. As she walked, she untwined her hair. Perhaps loose, it would hide her imperfections. What must he think of her, skinny and pock-marked?

Hester, who met Caylan with a gracious kiss on the cheek, only looked all the more ethereal for her thinness. After assuring Jenny that Liberty was down for a nap, Hester set out cider and bread for the Highlander before sitting across from him.

Jenny's sister clasped her hands on the table. "Now tell us your business and why you come alone."

Caylan tore into the bread. They waited for him to chew and swallow a couple of bites—Jenny keeping her back angled from the sideboard as she wrapped the bread—before he answered. "On the fourteenth, we struck Augusta and took it with no trouble, but the British holed up in M'Kay's Trading Post outside town. We drove their Cherokee allies away from the spring they guarded, thinking to deprive them of water." As if that reminded him of his thirst, he gulped down the cider, wiping his mouth with his sleeve. "But Brown, whom we shot through both thighs, received word a large host of British were on the way and refused our offer of surrender."

Jenny turned to face him. "Brown? Thomas Brown, of Augusta?"

"Aye, lass. Ye've heard of him?"

She blew out a breath. "Who has not?"

"Indeed." Hester wobbled her chin up and down, then embellished with a delicate shudder. "Even I know who Burntfoot Brown is."

The seed of Brown's hatred for Patriots had been planted deep when the Loyalist farmer had refused to sign a Sons of Liberty Continental Association document. An angry mob had followed him home, tied him to a tree, deprived him of part of his scalp, and then tarred and feathered him. A blow to his head that fractured his skull had left him with a laudanum dependency, while the fire lit beneath his feet had left him with the moniker. Brown had fled to South Carolina, then to Florida, where he obtained a commission as lieutenant colonel of the Florida Rangers. 'Twas little wonder the man had since made it his sole aim to visit havoc upon the backcountry.

In times like these, often only a thin line distinguished friend from foe, hero from villain.

"Then you know what manner of commander we were facing." Caylan looked at them with strangely entreating eyes. "We had to pull back. Clark was wounded again, and we could not take such a force."

Hester touched his hand. "Of course."

He stared at her. "Ye understand this means all the state falls into British hands. We are being called the

Georgia Refugees, for all others have taken oaths of loyalty. Everyone is gathering at the Little River for militia escort to the Carolinas."

Jenny scoffed. "'Everyone' has fled before, but not us."

Caylan turned a blazing gaze on her as she laid roasted chestnuts and cheese before him. "'Tis different this time. No one will be left to come to yer aid. No men at Clark's Station or Fort Martin."

She crossed her arms. "We have held off both Indians and Tories before."

He stood, peering down at her. "With *help*, may I remind ye?"

"Fine, but what has Father to say?"

Caylan clenched his jaw. "I speak for him. 'Tis the only way, Jenny." That same sadness filled his gaze, making her soften.

Hester lifted her chin. "How long do we have?"

"I need ye packed and ready to go in under an hour. I already passed word to Mrs. Clark that her husband was wounded again at Augusta, and she rides ahead to camp. We shall cut across country to the rendezvous."

Jenny did not comply with grace. She banged, stomped, and muttered about the sure demise of their home without their occupancy. It burned her heart to leave the corn standing in the field, the clothes unspun from waiting flax.

They packed oilcloth, quilts, and as much foodstuffs as the packs Caylan prepared on the horses would carry. She could not hide the tears in her eyes as she and Caylan surveyed the stockade.

"I am sorry, Jenny." He held his stallion's reins and glanced at Hester holding Liberty's hand. "Hester should ride with me, and the wee one with Jenny."

Because Jenny was big and heavy. Of course. She huffed into Merry's saddle and took her sister from Caylan's hands, then averted her gaze as he mounted his stallion and helped Hester up. Hester's blushing response to the Highlander's nearness told Jenny her sister was not over Caylan. Jealousy coiled like a serpent in Jenny's belly. She would ride ahead if only Caylan did not need to show them the way.

As they traveled southeast along an Indian trail, the tang of smoke filled the late-September air. "Clark's Station, I reckon," Caylan said over his shoulder.

Jenny suppressed a groan. How long before whatever miscreants started that blaze set fire to Fort White? Years of back-breaking labor—whole families' dreams—could disappear in an instant on this frontier.

The land lay in familiar patterns as they approached the main road to Kettle Creek. A shot rang out up ahead, and Caylan instructed them to wait in the woods while he investigated. Jenny pressed a cloth doll into Liberty's hands and urged her to silence.

Minutes later, he whistled, and they rode on to join him.

On the side of the narrow lane, Caylan spoke with a black man and Hannah Clark, both on horseback. Jenny spurred Merry closer. The colonel's wife handed Caylan a basket containing her infant twins from the front of her saddle, then allowed him to help her down. Blood trailed from a wound on her mount's haunch.

"Mrs. Clark, are you all right?" Jenny cried.

"I am." Hannah wiped a tear from her eye. She pulled a roll of multi-colored material from behind her horse's saddle. "But take this quilt, too, Lieutenant, for we almost died saving it. My Sarah and Betsy sewed it. When the British tried to abscond with it, I got mad all over again thinking of those shirts they stole."

"You challenged British soldiers over a quilt?" Hester gasped.

Jenny nudged Merry close enough that she could take the bundle from Hannah, seeing as how Caylan's arms were still full of babies. Interestingly enough, he hadn't even looked up from their small faces. She tucked the quilt in front of Liberty.

The colonel's wife darted a ghost of a smile at Hester. "I'm afraid so. I didn't even think—just reacted. I'm so weary of being pushed around."

A low chuckle broke from Caylan's chest. "Sounds like someone else I know."

Jenny tossed her head. She could think of no woman more admirable to be compared to.

Hannah didn't appear to hear him, however, her attention on her twins as she took the basket back from Caylan. "Now I realize how careless that was." Her voice had gentled. "The Good Lord must've been looking out for me. One of the soldiers said a woman so brave should not be killed, so they let me go."

Hester made a soft, scoffing sound. "Must have been a better-bred bunch than those that came calling on us."

Hannah frowned at her mount's wound. "Yes, but now what?"

"You can ride with us, of course," Jenny offered.

"Thank you, but time is of the essence. I fear for my husband's life."

Her servant spoke up. "Take my horse, ma'am. I tend yours and catch up wid you at Little River."

Reluctantly, the colonel's wife agreed.

Soon Hannah was ready to go, the twins again secured in front of her, quilt behind, and Jenny said, "We pray you find your husband well."

"Yes, and that we will all be together in Watauga."

"Godspeed," said Caylan.

"Watauga?" Jenny turned round eyes on Caylan as Hannah sped across the road and continued east on the Indian path.

Caylan failed to meet her gaze as he remounted behind Hester. "Clark journeys to Fort Caswell at Sycamore Shoals. The settlers there bought land from the Cherokee in seventy-five outside the realm of any state, becoming Washington County, North Carolina, about the time the Cherokee, allied with the British, turned on them. They already repelled that invasion. 'Twill be a place of unquestionable safety."

Jenny fumed. "Yes, but one I never would have agreed to had I been informed! You said 'Carolinas.' I assumed we merely forded the Savannah."

"Well, that was your mistake." Caylan urged his stallion onto the trail opening between the golden trees.

Jenny followed on Merry, raising her voice. "That journey is impossibly far, slow with those on foot and children, and across a mountain range!"

"Aye. It could take a couple of weeks."

"'Tis insanity!"

"The Overmountain Men are the toughest bunch of settlers west of the Appalachians. 'Tis a wise choice." One narrowed eye glanced back over his broad shoulder. "Now shut yer clacker, woman. I am trying to save yer life, and all I get for it is complaint!"

Jenny pinched her lips together, horrified to feel tears smart in her eyes. Caylan had never spoken thus to her. His reactions confused her—tenderness, sadness, and anger. She had seen all in half a day. Likely, he now wished to throw them over but felt constrained by his Scottish chivalry. And why did it seem that he hid something from them?

When they paused after fording Fishing Creek for the horses to water, Caylan sidled up to her. "I apologize for snappin' earlier, lass."

She nibbled a piece of jerky and stared at the water. "'Tis of no account. You have been through much, and now are saddled with two women and a child."

Caylan drew in his lips. "I am not 'saddled.' I would ride through hell for ye. But I *am* angry at ye."

"But why?" she gasped.

"You tell me." His hand darted into his haversack. "What is *this*?"

As he shoved the clan brooch toward her, Jenny's lips parted. Her heart went *ker-thump,* then took a short break from its labor.

"When I found this in my pack after I left this spring, I could have wrung yer neck." His hot breath on her cheek—not to mention the heat behind his alarming choice of words—produced the opposite effect in her body, chilling her from head to toe. His eyes bored into hers. "What kind of coward breaks a pledge in such a fashion? And is that how ye meant it, to break with me?"

"I meant to—to release you."

"*Why*?"

"Because things have changed. *I* have changed."

"Ye mean the pox."

Jenny swallowed. "Another sort of girl would suit you better." One such as Hester.

"Will ye let *me* decide that?" As Hester approached, Caylan slid the pin back into his bag and stood. "We must go now, but we are not done with this discussion." He raised his voice to include her sister. "We should make better time when we reach the other road toward Wrightsboro."

Jenny set aside her angst. "The Quaker settlement?"

"Aye. Their town lies about thirty-five miles north-northwest of Augusta. When we camp tonight, I must tell you both important news."

---

*C*rickets sang and Liberty whimpered by the time they smelled smoke. Dozens of tiny fires licked the russet evening around the millhouse chosen as the gathering point. Jenny could not believe the number of people present, bedraggled and starved settlers fleeing their homeland.

Leading their horses toward one of the first clusters,

they were surprised to see one of the Morris brothers and Philip Dunst, who had visited in January of seventy-nine. Philip's short, round mother, Gertie, and several younger siblings accompanied him. All bade Caylan and the Whites to partake of their cornbread and fish.

Jenny's stomach rumbled, but she said, "Thank you, but we really must find Father and Gabriel." The look of confusion she intercepted from Gertie dissolved into pity as Liberty plunked down next to the Dunst youngest and started scooping fish off a platter with her fingers.

"The wee bairn's famished. Let her eat." Caylan helped Hester, wobbly from unaccustomed hours in the saddle, to a log. She gave him a grateful smile for the corn pone he placed in her hand.

Jenny lowered herself with unwilling exhaustion onto the ground next to Morris. Mayhap the war and the loss of his brother had softened him, for he offered her a nod and even a hint of a smile. Did she look that bad? She ducked her head and thanked Mrs. Dunst for the victuals.

"Has the route been discussed?" Caylan lounged beside Philip, extending his long legs toward the fire.

"We parallel the river up to a crossing below the Tugaloo, as soon as Clark is fit to ride."

Morris shook his head. "No one's survived more wounds than Clark. He shall be back in the saddle by tomorrow, I wager. I don't think he was bad off—leastways, not as bad as those we had to leave behind." He cast a regretful glance over Jenny and Hester.

Vexed with the man's staring, Jenny set down her plate. "What?" she demanded.

"Nothing, I am just sorry for you."

"Have you never seen a pox victim before? When I leave the campfire, are you going to call me names again as you did at my home?"

The whiplash curl of her words rendered the gathering silent. The dark-haired man spluttered, "'Twasn't your scars I referred to, and I would never speak ill at such a time."

"What do you mean?" Jenny searched the assembled faces, aware of an awkwardness she did not understand. Caylan especially looked pained.

Gertie laid a plump hand on his arm. "Have you not told them, Caylan?"

Hester gasped. "Told us what?" From her expression, Jenny knew her sister's heart pounded like her own, and a damp chill not from the river swirled up to envelop her.

Gertie waddled over to sit next to Hester, placing an arm around her and meeting Jenny's stricken gaze across the fire. "Girls, your father fell at Cedar Spring back in July, and your brother..." She paused and sought Caylan's reaction. His frown, strangely warning, seemed to demand something of her. She finished with abrupt simplicity. "Your brother was a casualty of the Indians in Augusta."

CHAPTER 8

*C*aylan attempted to comfort her, but Jenny's anger would not allow it. How could he have lured them from home by trickery and deceit? She avoided him. It was easy enough to do as the mass of people moved along Indian paths through primeval forests, escorted by the militia. Her anger provided a useful shield against deeper emotions of shock, loss, and terror. What would they do when this exodus ended, having no menfolk or parent to return home with? Whoever heard of three women living alone on the frontier? And who would ever want her—gangly, starved, and scarred, with two younger sisters in tow? Even Caylan could not wish for such a package.

Jenny tried to push these thoughts from her mind. She committed herself to seeking provisions and carrying Liberty, but sensing Jenny's hardness, the child whined for Hester.

Unlike Jenny, Hester allowed her tears to flow unchecked. Not a complaint passed her lips, and receiving comfort from strangers, she started deep friendships. The new, stronger Hester was the prize Caylan deserved.

The few provisions brought from home ran out soon after they crossed the Savannah River. The people foraged for berries, nuts, wild greens, mushrooms, and sour crabapples. They hunted for wildlife, but there was never enough to go around. There must be at least four hundred civilians under the escort of Clark's three hundred. There was no time for dawdling by campfires, for they heard Patrick Ferguson's men pursued under Lord Cornwallis's orders.

One afternoon in the rolling hills of South Carolina, they paused along a stream. Jenny splashed her face with water and looked up to find Hester watching her.

"You do not grieve Father and Gabriel." Pity lined her sister's smooth features. "'Tis not healthy. You must soon face our loss, sister."

"I feel it. I feel it in *here*." Jenny struck her breast.

"Yes, but you must let it out, or you will explode." Her sister lowered herself onto a moss-covered rock, leaning forward. "And why do you keep Caylan at arm's length?"

DENISE WEIMER

"Because he tricked us, Hester. He did not trust us enough to tell us the truth."

"Is that really why?"

Jenny shook her head and stood up, gazing at Gertie's children as they played on the bank. "Liberty?" She saw the child nowhere. Jenny's heart rate picked up. "Liberty!"

Gertie stepped forward, clasping her hands together. "Oh, dear, I am sorry. I thought you had her."

Jenny shot an accusing glance at Hester, then sprang into the woods, calling the girl's name. She caught a glimpse of striped linen on the other side of a thick evergreen shrub...a hawthorn bush. Cold dread engulfed her. When she caught Libby in her arms, the child clutched a handful of the blue-black berries, while a corresponding stain colored her lips.

She thrust her fingers into her sister's mouth. "Spit it out! Did you eat the seeds?" Liberty choked, spit, and started to cry. Several adults rushed up as Jenny demanded, "Did you eat any before those?"

The girl shook her head, letting her handful of tiny fruit fall to the forest floor.

Jenny jostled her by the shoulders. "I told you to eat *no* berries without asking first!"

"I forgot," Libby sobbed.

"We can eat hawthorn berries, but we must spit out

104

the seeds. And the thorns are as long as your hand and cut like knives!"

Caylan touched Jenny's shoulder and called her name. "Leave off. Ye frighten the lass."

"I mean to frighten her! She could have died!" Jenny pinched her sister's arm, but Hester swooped in and took Liberty up.

"'Tis fine now, Jenny. She shan't forget again." With a censoring frown, Hester walked back toward the creek.

Shamed by the stares and the powerful fear that gripped her more strongly than she had gripped Liberty, Jenny covered her face. "I do not know what is wrong with me."

"I do. Ye're rightfully terrified of losing someone else you love."

"Yes," Jenny admitted as the group around them dispersed in silent understanding. "I am afraid I shall be left with none of the family I came to Georgia with."

"Ye won't. And ye have me."

When he tried to touch her, she pushed him away and fled downstream, fearing the imminent eruption of emotion. She leaned against a massive black oak. Above her shallow breaths, the voices of two women carried from across the narrow stream.

"'Tis understandable," one said. "The poor thing's addlepated, and who can blame her? Having lost her father and brother all in one blow, her mother just last fall."

"Aye," a second woman agreed. "And to such an awful fate, Gabriel White. Law, for a brave, wounded young man like that to be left to the mercy of the enemy! They say that monster Brown had thirteen of the prisoners hung from the banister where he could see them expire from his sickbed. Then cut down and given to the Indians to be mutilated and thrown into the river."

"The others went straight to the Indians, scalped and roasted."

With a moan of agony, Jenny leaned over and retched up the thin juices of her stomach.

Caylan found her doubled over, gasping. "What is it, Jenny?"

She speared him with her eyes. "Is it true?"

"Is what true?"

"That not only did you deceive us into thinking Father and Gabriel waited for us in camp—"

"I never said that."

"But Gabriel was left with the wounded in Augusta, to be tortured by Indians?"

Caylan's bronzed face paled. "Where did ye hear that?"

Jenny nodded across the creek. "I overheard them

just now. So it is true." When he remained silent, she shook her head and tried to walk past him.

His hand snaked out to grip her elbow.

"Do not touch me." When Caylan persisted in trying to pull her into his arms, Jenny fought, slapped, and wriggled.

"Stop it, lass. I can see how ye are hurting. Ye must stop this running."

She pounded his chest with her fists, hard. "How could you not tell me? How could you leave me to hear something like that from prattling strangers?"

"Oh, Jenny, I am sorry. I was going to tell ye, just when we reached the mountains. When we had time to...deal with it all." Caylan wrapped his fingers around her wrists but kept the other arm anchored on her waist. "I knew ye would fight me on leaving if ye thought they were not waiting at the river. And I only held back the details about yer brother because I knew 'twould pain ye so."

Picturing the awful scene described by the women, Jenny choked on horror, her heart rending for her young brother. "Oh, God, 'tisn't fair!" she wailed.

Caylan released her wrists and ran his fingers through her hair. He breathed against her cheek. "Let it out, lass. We all have a breaking point, even ye."

Alarmed at the wild and tortured sounds coming out of herself, Jenny buried her face in Caylan's overcoat. He wrapped both arms around her and murmured words that must be Gaelic, but they sounded ever so sweet. When her knees crumpled, he held her up. When people started to move down the trail, he stroked her back.

Finally, as her sobs quieted to moans and gasps, he murmured, "Look at me, lass."

No fight left in her, she raised her face with her closed eyes still streaming tears.

"Ye have suffered more than any woman ought, and been braver and stronger far longer than ye should have had to be." He began to kiss the tears away.

She shuddered as his tender lips contacted her dimpled flesh. "Do not," Jenny whispered.

"Nae, lass, dinna shrink from me. What kind of blackguard do ye think me, to consider leaving ye alone now?"

"Not a blackguard at all. 'Tis why I released you."

"Well, I refuse your release." His mouth skimmed hers, seeking response.

Jenny turned her head. "I am not worthy of you now."

"Does that mean ye forgive me?"

She dropped her arms, stepping back from him, and said in a spent tone, "Yes. I know what you did was for our own good. And you were right, had you told me then what I know now, you would never have gotten me to leave Fort White."

"Then what is it? Why are ye not worthy?" When she only shook her head, Caylan dug in his haversack. "Is it the way ye look? Because I took this shaving mirror off a dead Brit, expressly to refute yer protests."

"No!"

He shoved it into her hand and held her hand up to her face. "Look, Jenny. See what I see."

Jenny dragged a sleeve across her cheeks and gazed at the first clear reflection she had seen of herself since age thirteen. The woman who stared back lacked the heavy features of adolescence she recalled. Maturity and starvation revealed fine, strong bones, almost noble, framed by a wildness of russet hair, with damp dark-brown lashes. The pox indentations were visible, true, but slight. Her brother had been right. The scattering of freckles across her nose drew attention to her eyes...eyes the very color of Caylan's.

Her hand started to shake.

Caylan caught the mirror before she dropped it. He drew her against him. "Will ye kiss me now, Jenny, my love? Wahatchee."

Finally, War Woman surrendered.

*T*hat night, Jenny lay by the campfire in Caylan's arms, facing her little sister as Liberty snuggled between herself and Hester. The oilcloth beneath them rustled against leaves as Caylan nestled closer, brushing her ear with his lips.

"Kiss me again as ye did before," he whispered.

"No, you devil," Jenny hissed. "My sisters! And all these people!"

At his soft, frustrated growl, Jenny sucked in a breath. She did not trust herself to turn and face him. It was a testament to the power of her attraction that her exhaustion had not triumphed by culminating in sleep the minute she laid down.

His fingers twined in her hair, and Jenny closed her eyes. How long she had coveted such a tender touch.

"Ye know I love ye, don't ye, lass?" The soft words made her breath freeze in her throat.

She swiveled her head to stare at him, but the darkness lay too heavy on his features for her to read them. Her blood rushed through her veins like a spring freshet down the mountain.

He dipped his forehead to hers. "Let me say it again, and let there be no teasing in my tone." Indeed, the wheedling charm that was so his way disappeared. His voice deepened, roughened at the edges. "I love ye,

Jenny White. There is no other woman in the world for me but you."

Breath trembling over her lips, Jenny raised her hand to his head. She would be a fool to question words spoken in that tone. "I love you, too, Caylan. So much, it terrifies me."

He chuckled low. "'Twouldn't be love for people such as us if there wasn't enough passion in it to terrify."

Lifting her chin, she pressed his face closer and her parted lips to his. He kissed her with a thoroughness that made her heart soar. She was wanted. Not only that —she was chosen.

Only when his hand dropped to her waist to draw her closer did she remember her sisters on her other side. "Caylan," she whispered. "This is why I denied you earlier."

He uttered a soft groan but allowed her to put a few inches between them. Still, he traced the ridges of her face with a trembling finger. "I say the time for denying should be long past. I've heard there's a justice of the peace in our company. Should I go wake him?" His unsteady laugh told her he was only half joking.

Jenny propped her hand on her hip and grinned like a fool in the darkness. "And what shall you say to him that you have failed to say to me?" Her teasing question came out thick with joy.

"By the saints! I plumb forgot to ask." Caylan gathered her hand between his and held it to his chest. "If ye will forgive this unconventional proposal, Miss White, I ask ye with all my heart to marry me."

"I will, Caylan McIntosh. As soon as we reach Fort Caswell." She added the last lest he leap up from their pallet and go in search of the official.

He let out a gust of breath. "Praise be. And ye willna go back on it?"

She mimicked his brogue. "I willna go back on it."

They dissolved into soft laughter, earning Hester's shushing. But even her sister's rebuke could not squelch the joy that bubbled like a fresh spring inside Jenny. They settled with her back to Caylan again, his arm over her. She fell asleep listening to his deep breathing and feeling the rise and fall of his chest at her back, a song in her heart that whispered comfort over her grief.

———

*T*he next day, one of the runners Clark had sent ahead to Watauga with notice of their approach returned from the river settlement, asking to speak to the commander. Jenny watched from a distance as the handsome, dark-haired colonel in his buff-and-navy uniform consulted with the North

Carolinian. Moments later, Caylan strode toward Jenny and Hester.

"The Overmountain Men gathered at Fort Caswell on the twenty-fifth. Hearing of Ferguson's threat to hang their leaders and lay waste to their country with fire and sword, they marched out to meet him. Major Candler and volunteers from our regiment will rendezvous with them on the Green River."

"But not you." Jenny's lips went numb as she spoke. *Please.*

"With such powerful allies, this could end the war in the south."

Jenny's panic surged at the struggle writ on Caylan's face. Pride attempted to silence her, but she forced the words out. Caylan drew near, clasping her elbows as she spoke. "If you leave with them, I think I will not see you again. And I could not bear that, Caylan. I have only just accepted that I do need God, others...you."

He looked deep into her eyes. "Ye're outright askin' me to stay, Jenny?"

"I am. Please go with us to Sycamore Shoals."

Did he know what that cost her?

He did. With a heavy exhale, he crushed her to his chest. "I shan't abandon ye when I just pledged to stay by ye." At his declaration, a sob stole from Jenny's throat. He kissed the top of her head. "I can rejoin the fight when Clark returns to Georgia, for return he shall. But...will ye marry me now?"

Jenny's eyes opened wide. "Now?"

"Aye. Now. Here." He flung a long arm out toward a magnificent outcropping of rock overlooking a breath-taking mountain vista. "I canna think of a more fitting place to make ye my bride."

Nor could Jenny. She laughed while the Georgia Refugees, gathered around and watching them with expressions of rapt interest and delight, broke into applause.

"I take that as a yes." Caylan turned to search the crowd. "Now where is the justice of the peace?"

~THE END~

AUTHOR'S NOTE

A Courageous Betrothal was originally published as *Across Three Autumns* in Barbour's Backcountry Brides Collection (2018). I'm so delighted it's being released again as a bonus novella with Wild Heart Books as part of the Scouts of the Georgia Frontier Series. While our hero, Caylan, was completely fictional, its heroine was inspired by Nancy Hart and her famous exploits against the British and Indians when the borderlands of Georgia were known as "the Hornet's Nest" during the American Revolution.

Nancy Ann Morgan Hart moved from North Carolina to the Broad River—Elbert County, Georgia—in the early 1770s. With her husband, Benjamin, who became a lieutenant under Colonel Elijah Clark, she raised six sons and two daughters. But Nancy was not the expected meek Colonial woman. Pipe-smoking, crossed-eyed, and pock-marked, six-foot-tall Nancy was a crack shot the Indians called "Wahatche" or "War Woman," and named the creek on her property after her.

During the British occupation of Augusta, when Colonel Clark needed information on enemy plans, Nancy dressed as a man and pretended to be "addle-pated" to gain confidences in the British camp.

Other exploits were echoed in *A Courageous Betrothal*. While Nancy was making soap over the fire, one of her children noticed an eye peeking in the cabin chinking. Nancy threw lye into the crevice and went outside to hog-tie and take the prisoner to local militia. Another time, when Nancy dressed as a sick woman and misdirected six British soldiers in their pursuit of a rebel, they shot her last turkey and insisted she cook it for them. Nancy broke out the corn liquor and sent her daughter Sukey to the swamp ostensibly to get water but really to blow a conch shell to summon her father and neighbors working in a far field. Meanwhile, Nancy passed the soldiers' stacked weapons through a chink in the wall. She got caught on the third. Nancy leveled the musket and warned the men she'd shoot any who advanced. One made that mistake and was rapidly dispatched. The others froze, convinced, and also quite confused by Nancy's roving eye as to who her next target might be. She held the others at bay until help arrived, then insisted shooting was too good for the interlopers. Legend says the settlers hung the party of British. In 1912, a railroad grading crew uncovered six skeletons under three feet of Hart dirt, giving credence to this particular story.

Nancy's later days had a good ending. Governor George Gilmer's mother testified late in life that Nancy "went to the house of worship in search of relief." Cutting the fastening off the door of the Methodist meeting house, Nancy barged in and stated she'd heard how the wicked might work out their salvation. "She ... became a shouting Christian, [and] fought the devil as manfully as she had fought the Tories."

The stories about Mammy Kate, Hannah Harrington Clark, and Thomas "Burntfoot" Brown were also true. The backcountry of the Colonies during the Revolution produced both unspeakable atrocities and the kind of bravery that birthed legends.

Wondering what happened to the Georgia Refugees? The Southern Colonists scored a decisive victory against the British at the Battle of King's Mountain, North Carolina, on October 7, 1780. Colonel Clark's men went on to fight at Blackstock's Farm in November and Long Cane Creek, South Carolina, in December, where he was wounded in the shoulder. He returned to Georgia, his troops dispersing until spring. In April of 1781, Clark and his militia reactivated in the Georgia backcountry to harass loyalists and threaten British-held Augusta. They found that in their absence, homes had been burned, aged relatives arrested, and women in the refugee camps had been robbed and abused.

In May of 1781, Clark joined Major General Nathanael Greene and Lieutenant Colonel "Lighthorse Harry" Lee in the siege of Augusta. Lee's engineers constructed a wooden tower from which a cannonball could reach the interior of Fort Cornwallis. Lieutenant Colonel Thomas Brown surrendered the city on June 5, 1781, clearing the way for the Georgia Refugees to return home. The Patriot seizure of Augusta also gave American peace negotiators in Paris reason to demand the independence of Georgia even though Savannah remained in British hands for the ensuing year of war. The scattered members of the Georgia legislature reassembled in August in Augusta.

ABOUT THE AUTHOR

North Georgia native Denise Weimer has authored over a dozen traditionally published novels and a number of novellas—historical and contemporary romance, romantic suspense, and time slip. As a freelance editor and Acquisitions & Editorial Liaison for Wild Heart Books, she's helped other authors reach their publishing dreams. A wife and mother of two daughters, Denise always pauses for coffee, chocolate, and old houses.

Connect with Denise here:

Monthly Newsletter Sign-up: http://eepurl.com/dFfSfn

Website: https://deniseweimerbooks.webs.com/

BookBub: https://www.bookbub.com/profile/denise-weimer

Facebook: facebook.com/denise.weimer1

X: twitter.com/denise_weimer

Did you enjoy this book? We hope so!
**Would you take a quick minute to leave a review
where you purchased the book?**
It doesn't have to be long. Just a sentence or two telling
what you liked about the story!

———————

Receive a FREE ebook and get updates when new Wild
Heart books release: https://wildheartbooks.org/
newsletter

Don't miss the next book in The Scouts of the Georgia Frontier Series!

A Cherished Betrothal

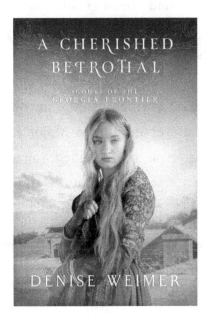

JULY 12, 1775
FORT CHARLOTTE, SOUTH CAROLINA

"Dinna touch me, sir!"

The sharp command from the captain's residence stopped Lieutenant Alexander Morris in the process of striking the British colors in the fort's yard. The act itself had already given him pause, for there could be no going back from this. The taking of a crown fort—

even one in the backcountry—was no less an act of aggression for the lack of bloodshed.

But what was a Scottish woman—unmistakable, from her lilting brogue—doing here?

Alex's men had been instructed to supervise Captain George Whitefield's family as they packed and prepared to be escorted from Fort Charlotte. A wagon awaited them with horses already hitched in the yard. They would travel northeast to the town of Ninety Six, along with whatever munitions Major James Mayson chose to transfer to the fortified town. Where the Whitefields went from there mattered not, so long as—having refused to join the Patriot cause—they left the area.

The undeniable rumble of an argument proceeded through the open door of the captain's quarters. Alex folded the flag over his arm, smoothing the King's Colours with his scarred hand. He'd fought with the Georgia Rangers under this banner, but never again. The line had been crossed now. Swallowing past the unexpected tightness in his throat, he pivoted and went to see what might be out of kilter with the Whitefields.

He was about to enter the captain's cabin when a petite form in a blue bodice and linen petticoat swept through the door, nearly colliding with him. The young woman stopped, one hand flying up to secure her tilting straw hat.

Alex made a small bow. "What seems to be the problem, lass?"

"Miss Lawrence," Sergeant Sean McTavish supplied. He stood behind her, his ginger-bearded face a thundercloud above his blue coat with red facings. "We found her visiting with Mrs. Whitefield and more than a bit contrary about takin' her leave."

Lawrence. Now, why was that name familiar, like a moth tickling about the edges of his recollection?

"I'm not contrary. I only wanted to say a prayer." Miss Lawrence lifted moist blue eyes to Alex's, blinked, and sucked in a breath. She peered at him, no doubt catching sight of the edge of the scar that ran from beneath his cocked hat to the tip of his left eyebrow.

Alex was well-accustomed to people staring, but somehow, this woman's perusal shortened his patience —not his best quality even on a good day. "Prayer?"

"For safety for the Whitefields' journey. I was only askin' for one last, peaceful moment alone in their home, to cover them with the Lord's protection."

"And I told her, we don't need no Loyalist prayers. We'd thankee to mount yer horse." Sergeant McTavish leaned the tip of his rifle toward the extra mounts at the hitching post. "We willna keep the major waiting."

"Let her have her prayer, Sergeant," Alex said.

When Miss Lawrence's full pink lips parted, he gestured toward the doorway.

"Thankee, sir," she whispered. "Lieutenant...?"

No call to further this acquaintance. Even had he been assigned here at Fort Charlotte rather than the town of Ninety Six, he possessed no skill with ladies. Nor the desire to develop it. Alex stuck his head into the cabin and ordered the remaining privates away. "The Whitefield family wishes a moment of reflection before they depart."

After the men scrambled out, squinting against the bright sunshine, Miss Lawrence entered and crossed to Mrs. Whitefield, who clasped her bairn to her bosom while a toddler clung to the leg of the English captain. The three joined hands, and Alex waited only long enough for Miss Lawrence to begin in a quavering voice, "Most merciful God..." before himself stepping outside.

Sergeant McTavish scowled at him. "A cryin' shame, a sawny lass hand in glove with Loyalists."

"Why is she here on her own, anyway? Where does she come from?" Alex wiped his forehead with his sleeve and surveyed the fifty-by-forty, four-bastioned enclosure, which swarmed with blue-coated men. Barrels of gunpowder and ammunition were being hefted onto wagons and two small brass field pieces secured on carriages. The full-sized guns would remain, though a want of platforms and working caissons made them somewhat redundant. The stone fort had cost a thousand pounds sterling to construct a decade before but now greatly needed repair.

"She said her father is the minister at the Presbyterian mission just north of here on Russell's Creek."

It was Alex's turn to frown. "Aren't most parsons in these parts itinerant?"

"Not this one. Apparently, Reverend Lawrence has been holdin' services for the British soldiers at the fort as well as for our countrymen in these parts. And they say they have Cherokee children at the mission."

Alex's face went slack, and McTavish gave a grim nod. Fort Charlotte might be the colony's westernmost outpost on the Savannah River, but he hadn't expected a reason for an enemy more dangerous than the Loyalists to regularly come and go.

"Lieutenant Morris." Alex's captain, Moses Kirkland, strode toward them, his brow set in a harsh line. "Where are the Whitefields? Our company has assembled, and Major Mayson is waiting to mount up." Captain Kirkland jerked his chin toward the parade ground, where their commanding officer inspected the cannons.

"I will fetch them, sir." Indeed, they would need every bit of light for their lumbering party to reach Ninety Six—named for its distance from the important Cherokee town of Keowee—before dark, even on this mid-summer day.

Sergeant McTavish pulled a face. "They needed to say their prayers first, sir."

Captain Kirkland scoffed. "They will need them. Round them up, Lieutenant Morris, with no further mollycoddling."

Kirkland's tone—brusque as ever—rankled Alex. How much of the man's current distemper stemmed from losing the appointment of major to Mayson? Alex might regret heeding his cousin Finn's invitation to sign up under this particular former Regulator, but he'd let nothing interfere with his chance to prove himself in a worthy cause. He belonged here, in uniform. Not behind a plow in Georgia's recently ceded lands. He saluted, then handed the flag to the captain. "As requested—the King's Colours."

Though the Patriots had no banner as yet to fly in its place, Major Mayson would present the British flag to Captain Whitefield to carry with him to his own commander.

Kirkland snatched the folded bundle and pivoted for the parade ground.

In the dim interior of the captain's quarters, Alex found Captain Whitefield latching a traveling trunk while the women embraced. Frances Whitefield wept softly. "You have been a kindly friend for me in this lonely place, Elspeth."

Elspeth...so that was the name of this lass with flaxen-blond hair such as he hadn't seen since...

"And you to me." Dropping Frances's hands, Miss Lawrence glanced at him.

Alex cleared his throat and addressed Captain Whitefield. "Sir, Major Mayson awaits yer presence on the parade ground. Some of my privates will fetch yer luggage."

Alex's refusal to remove his hat might be marked as a lack of respect, but he couldn't bring himself to do so under the watchful gaze of Miss Lawrence. To track the disintegration of her poorly concealed interest from shock, to horror, and finally, pity—a reaction he'd witnessed too many times. And that made him as irritable as Captain Kirkland. What cared he what this prim miss thought?

If he was offended, Captain Whitefield gave no indication. He straightened with a sigh, almost seeming resigned. Did he share their Patriot leanings, as some suspected? Was that why he hadn't fought back when Major Mayson had demanded the surrender of the fort?

Whitefield set his cocked hat atop his gray wig, as immaculate in his red coat, white breeches, and black boots as if he were conducting a review of His Majesty's troops rather than surrendering barely more than a dozen men to a foe His Majesty did not even recognize.

"Thank you, Lieutenant. Come, ladies." He gestured for the women to proceed him from the cabin.

Outside, the formal surrender took place in the fort's yard while Alex and his men assisted the civilians. After loading the Whitefields' luggage onto a supply wagon, Alex helped the captain's wife and toddler girl into the back. Miss Lawrence handed Mrs. Whitefield her baby boy, then turned to look at him.

"Do one of the mounts here belong to you, miss?" he asked.

"No, sir. My father has our horse. He left me here to visit Mrs. Whitefield while he went to call on a friend in New Bordeaux."

At least that satisfied his concern that this beautiful young woman's father would allow her to traipse across the countryside on her own. "Very good. New Bordeaux is along our route to Ninety Six. We will drop you off there."

She hesitated. Surely, she was not thinking of awaiting the reverend's return at a fort occupied by strangers, without another woman or chaperone. "Are you going? To Ninety Six?"

Her question brought him up short. "Aye, miss. That is where I've been posted. Now, please, allow me..." He held out his hand.

She took it, but rather than climbing into the wagon, she stepped closer to him "Lieutenant, what is yer name?" The question was barely above a whisper. Her blue eyes bore into his, tugging at something long furled up in his memory. Something he wanted to keep that way.

"Why would ye need me name?"

"Because I think I ken you. I think we...grew up together." The heat from her small fingers just might burn holes through Alex's white gloves.

Despite the momentous surrender of the fort taking place only yards away—the result of the first act of aggression by rebel armies on South Carolina soil—Mrs. Whitefield and Alex's men all stared at him and this strange Scottish lass. He sought to dispel their interest with a soft, scoffing breath and a tight smile.

"That canna be the case, for I have no memory of ye." And he certainly would, did he ken her.

Confusion, followed by what appeared to be deep disappointment, swam in her eyes. Then, before he could register her intent, she swiped his hat off his head. A dark, sweaty lock of hair fell loose from his queue, though it wasn't enough to cover his scars, judging by the flash of emotion on Miss Lawrence's face. But it wasn't the pity he expected. It was the most intense joy he'd ever seen, twisting his gut into a paroxysm of longing and alarm.

"It *is* ye." A small sob bubbled from her lips, and she

released his hand to cover it at the same moment she dropped his hat—and slumped toward the ground.

Alex. Alex. Alex.

Elspeth's mind repeated the name she'd once awakened from her nightmares calling out but which her faint heart lacked the strength to give voice, even now, as she jostled along in the wagon with her head pillowed on Frances's shoulder. Could it be? From the moment she'd noted the proud grace with which the man carried his lanky body, the set of his jaw, those eyes almost like coals, her heart had thundered. Her palms had grown sweaty, and her knees had shaken. And then, his Scottish brogue, so much deeper but still so musical—

"Elspeth, are you well?" Frances jostled her arm. No doubt the woman wanted back the one patch of herself not taken up with a slobbering babe or clinging toddler.

Elspeth sat upright, running her hand over her eyes. But the gesture did not clear the sight of the man riding his bay stallion behind the wagon, frowning in her direction. *Great God in heaven, could Ye have heard my prayer after all this time?* And was she about to be parted from the boy she'd sought for years, before he would even acknowledge her? Tell her his story?

The possibility seized her with such panic, she clutched her middle.

"Are you about to cast up your accounts?" Frances looked around, presumably for a vessel. "'Twould not be unusual, after a faint."

Elspeth stopped the woman's search with a hand on her elbow. "I dinna faint. I only went a wee bit dizzy." Although she possessed only the fuzziest memory of the lieutenant scooping her up and lifting her into the wagon, a spectacle for all to see.

Frances gave a light shudder. "No wonder, given the sight of that man's scars. Such fearsome damage could only have been done at the hands of the Indians."

"They were not so bad, the scars." Indeed, his hair had covered most, and they were healed to silver-white and old—fifteen years old, to be exact. But the tightening of her fingers on the edge of the wagon gave the lie to her words. The scars might not be bad now, but that day...

She pressed back a groan and shut the lid on the memory as solidly as she had on the chest of her dead mother's belongings that still sat at the foot of her father's bed.

Frances eased forward, into Elspeth's view. "And do you know him, as you thought?"

"I do." The confirmation of his name would punctuate her statement, though. She still hadn't heard it. And still couldn't speak it.

"From Long Canes Creek?" Frances knew Elspeth's story, the rare-spoken name of the place where she'd lost all family save Da, and she said it even now in the softest tone, almost looking apologetic. But intensely curious, just the same.

Elspeth drew breath to reply, but instead, a demand rang out from the head of the column. "Halt! What is the meaning of this? Where are you taking munitions that belong to the king?"

Major Mayson's reply reached them with equal clarity. "These munitions now belong to the provincial government of South Carolina, as does Fort Charlotte, from whence they came."

As their wagon rumbled to a stop, she raised herself in its bed for a view of whomever confronted Major Mayson, his adjutant, and Kirkland—the unpleasant, corpulent fellow whose troop now escorted them while the other captain of the South Carolina Regiment of Horse, Caldwell, remained with his company at Fort Charlotte. Captain Whitefield rode his stallion beside the Patriot officers. And now, a knot of mounted men in civilian clothing blocked the road leading into New Bordeaux—and not the French Huguenots who lived there.

Frances had swiveled around in the wagon. "Who is it?"

"Friends of yer husband's, I believe." She recognized the Cunningham brothers, Robert and Patrick, as well as Jacob Bowman, all of whom were outspoken proponents of King George.

Frances squeezed her hand. "Pray God there is not trouble."

Indeed, the lieutenant Elspeth believed was Alex had circled his men around their wagon even as they spoke. He leaned closer from the back of his horse, saying in a hiss, "Get down."

For a moment, she met his eyes, searching for some sign of recognition, some connection, but his were blank...though they narrowed.

"Sit...down...*miss*."

She was just about to do so when an agitated voice called her name. "Elspeth?"

She whirled around. "Da?" What was he doing here?

Mounted on his gelding, her father edged up the side of the road past the Cunningham brothers. "Oh, thank God, 'tis me daughter! Ye must let me reach her. She has no business in all this."

He sounded all affright. When Elspeth raised the hem of her petticoat in preparation to step onto the wagon wheel and jump down, Alex's hand landed firmly on her shoulder.

He jerked his chin at her. "'Twould be foolish to get in the middle of this confrontation. We ken not where it will lead."

"He is right, Elspeth." Frances patted the rough board next to her. "Sit here while they talk."

Elspeth sank between little Betsy and her mother. The toddler sucked her thumb. The drawn lines of her friend's face and the arm she wrapped around them both emphasized the danger only a few feet away. Would the Loyalists attempt to take the guns and powder by force? Had a battle been avoided at the fort only to break out on the road?

As her father said, she had no part in this. For years, they had successfully straddled the worlds of those who found fault with the king's governance, those who thought he'd done no wrong, and the Indians, both Creek and Cherokee. They'd focused on proclaiming the truth of God's love for all.

Would that fragile peace end here, today?

How foolish of her. It had already ended, the moment these newly recruited Patriot rangers had seized Fort Charlotte on orders of the provincial government's Council of Safety.

The firm, proud voices of the men carried to them for a few minutes, but Elspeth couldn't make out their words. At last, her father and an officer bearing more trim and fringe than Alex approached, faces tight.

Da reached out and grabbed her hand. "Elspeth, are ye well?"

"I'm fine, Da." But would her father recognize Alex? She nodded toward him, but he was saluting his superior.

"Adjutant," Alex greeted the man. "What's happening?"

"Given the presence of civilians, the Loyalists have agreed to avoid bloodshed, though a portion of the powder will be returned to Fort Charlotte. They think it less likely to create contention there, out of the way as it is."

Alex pressed his lips together. "I suppose they think we canna blow anything up without it." He turned to her. "And I suppose that means ye can hie home with yer father, Miss Lawrence."

"Actually, Lieutenant Morris..." The adjutant frowned and swiped his glistening brow. "Major Mayson wishes you to accompany the Lawrences to their mission and overnight with them."

"What?"

"Morris?" Elspeth's father broke in. "Alexander Morris?" He was looking at Alex much the way Elspeth imagined she had, leaning sideways to catch a glimpse under the cocked hat. "Why, is that really you, me boy?"

Alex's tanned cheeks had gone white. "That is me name, sir, but I fear ye share the same mistaken idea as yer daughter. I dinna ken ye."

Had Elspeth remained standing, her legs would have failed her. She grabbed Frances's hand, though the woman had no idea what this meant to her. Poor Frances allowed her to squeeze hard, though, not uttering a word.

"Yer father, he was Malcolm Morris, no?"

A brief nod was all the answer Alex gave, making Elspeth wish she could leap from the wagon and get her arms around him.

Thankfully, the adjutant gave a grunt and picked up the dangling thread of conversation. "Major Mayson heard the young lady recognized you. Reverend Lawrence told him he is expecting a small party of Cherokees."

"Aye, by tomorrow," Da confirmed.

Elspeth stiffened.

The young officer nodded, his steely gray eyes still on Alex, who kept his head down. "Reverend Lawrence will introduce you as his friend, Lieutenant Morris, and you will then issue an invitation for the Cherokees to visit Fort Charlotte on behalf of the provincial army. It is of the utmost importance to the major that the Cherokees know we are their friends."

If Elspeth had wanted to leap from the wagon

before, it was all she could do to stifle her moan of dismay now. Alex appeared far too stricken to utter any such protest himself—even if he had such a right while under orders. Could anything more difficult be asked of him? Had he even had dealings with the Indians these past years, as she had? Not likely—unless he'd met some of the Creeks in battle when they had last risen in Georgia, early the year prior.

"And if they willna come?" The words seemed to slide out through the lieutenant's stiff jaw.

The adjutant straightened. "Then you will join us in Ninety Six."

"And the reverend has agreed to this?"

Why did Alex ask the other officer, as though Da was not sitting right there?

Da, bless his heart, answered, anyway. "I have, Alex...er, Lieutenant Morris. My daughter and I will feel safer with ye at the mission while things are all arsy varsy. Besides, 'twill be good to catch up with ye."

"Verra well." Alex did not return his tentative smile. Instead, he saluted the adjutant. "Will that be all, sir?"

The man's mouth pursed, then he jerked his head toward a stand of pines nearby. Both men wheeled their horses in that direction and conferred in low tones. What was this about? Something they did not want her and Da to hear? And wasn't inserting their man at the mission—a supposedly neutral place—a way for the Patriots to nudge them into their camp?

"Come, Elspeth." Da drew his gelding next to the wagon and held his arm out.

Elspeth hugged Frances tightly. "Goodbye, my friend." She would dearly miss having a companion nearby. Indeed, having a female friend at all. In her experience, those were hard to come by.

"Goodbye, dear Elspeth. Keep safe. Write to me in Charlestown." Frances helped Elspeth cross the wagon wheel and get a leg over her father's mount while the men's backs were turned.

As she settled on the front of the saddle, she angled her body and whispered, "Da, can ye believe it? Is it really him?"

"Aye, lass, I think so, though for some reason, he doesna want us to ken that."

"Then why are ye allowin' him to come to the mission?"

"His major was verra suspicious of my appearance with the Loyalists." He spoke quickly, his tone low. "I crossed paths with them in Bordeaux and learned what was afoot. All I could think of was to get to you, my child. I would do anything to accomplish that."

She nodded. "I am glad ye're here."

"Besides, do ye not want to talk with him?"

Oh, more than anything. But would he talk?

The main column lumbered forward, the Loyalists having dispersed. Elspeth blew a kiss to Frances and little Betsy in the back of the wagon. The adjutant galloped off, and Alex Morris turned his horse their direction, his square, bristled jaw set, his eyes unreadable under the ever-tilted hat.

He was going home with them—the boy she'd longed to see for fifteen years. Yet he wasn't a boy any longer. He was a man, hardened and guarded. And either he was playing a part she had yet to grasp or he truly did not remember them. She couldn't decide which would be worse.

Want more?

If you love historical romance, check out the other Wild Heart books!

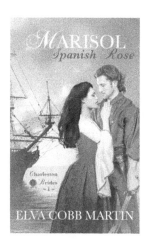

Marisol ~ Spanish Rose by Elva Cobb Martin

Escaping to the New World is her only option...Rescuing her will wrap the chains of the Inquisition around his neck.

Marisol Valentin flees Spain after murdering the nobleman who molested her. She ends up for sale on the indentured servants' block at Charles Town harbor —dirty, angry, and with child. Her hopes are shattered, but she must find a refuge for herself and the child she carries. Can this new land offer her the grace, love, and security she craves? Or must she escape again to her only living relative in Cartagena?

Captain Ethan Becket, once a Charles Town minister, now sails the seas as a privateer, grieving his deceased wife. But when he takes captive a ship full of indentured servants, he's intrigued by the woman whose manners seem much more refined than the average Spanish serving girl. Perfect to become governess for his young son. But when he sets out on a quest to find his captured sister, said to be in Cartagena, little does he expect his new Spanish governess to stow away on his ship with her six-month-old son. Yet her offer of help to free his sister is too tempting to pass up. And her beauty, both inside and out, is too attractive for his heart to protect itself against—until he learns she is a wanted murderess.

As their paths intertwine on a journey filled with danger, intrigue, and romance, only love and the grace of God can overcome the past and ignite a new beginning for Marisol and Ethan.

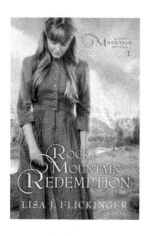

Rocky Mountain Redemption by Lisa J. Flickinger

A *Rocky Mountain* logging camp may be just the place to find herself.

To escape the devastation caused by the breaking of her wedding engagement, Isabelle Franklin joins her aunt in the Rocky Mountains to feed a camp of lumberjacks cutting on the slopes of Cougar Ridge. If only she could out run the lingering nightmares.

Charles Bailey, camp foreman and Stony Creek's itinerant pastor, develops a reputation to match his new nickname — Preach. However, an inner battle ensues when the details of his rough history threaten to overcome the beliefs of his young faith.

Amid the hazards of camp life, the unlikely friendship growing between the two surprises Isabelle. She's drawn to Preach's brute strength and gentle nature as he leads the ragtag crew toiling for Pollitt's Lumber. But when the ghosts from her past return to haunt her, the choices she will make change the course of her life forever—and that of the man she's come to love.

Lone Star Ranger by Renae Brumbaugh Green

Elizabeth Covington will get her man.

And she has just a week to prove her brother isn't the murderer Texas Ranger Rett Smith accuses him of being. She'll show the good-looking lawman he's wrong, even if it means setting out on a risky race across Texas to catch the real killer.

Rett doesn't want to convict an innocent man. But he can't let the Boston beauty sway his senses to set a guilty man free. When Elizabeth follows him on a dangerous trek, the Ranger vows to keep her safe. But who will protect him from the woman whose conviction and courage leave him doubting everything—even his heart?